The Hip-Hop Series

Word Works by, for and in the Language of the New Urban Generation

Www.PenknifePress.Com

More Boy Than Girl

More Boy Than Girl
by
Tony Lindsay

Penknife Press   Chicago, Illinois

This is a work of fiction. The characters, dialogue and events described herein are the products of the author's imagination, and do not portray actual persons or events.

ISBN 978-1-59997-007-3

Library of Congress Control Number: 2010942957

Manufactured in the United States of America

Acknowledgments

I would like to offer a special thanks to Larry Redmond of Penknife Press who said yes when others said no. And a heartfelt thank you to my close readers: Roy Mock, Will Palmer, Delores Thomas, and Cedric Young. Without y'all, Dai Break Jones would never have seen the light of day.

Chapter One

This ain't the time for a pimp to be laid up. It's too much going on in my life. This hospital situation is proof of that. Ain't a thug in my clique gonna believe a pimp fell out, and ended up flat on his back in this dump. Nope, no clique member or any of my ho'es gonna believe this here. Daisy really wouldn't believe it.

Daisy. . . Damn. I am going to miss that girl. I am gonna miss her deep. Out of the three of my ho'es she was the finest and the smartest. That's why she was my bottom.

When I first saw her, it was hard for me to believe she was a ho'e, because she looked so damn good. She was a dark, slim goody, with jet black hair that hung midway down her back. If she wasn't with a pimp, I would have thought she was an actress or singer or something. But she was a hundred percent ho'e, do whatever to whoever for them dollars, and ain't too many tricks on the strip can resist her swagger. As soon as she hit the bricks and got to switching that tight little butt of hers, she got picked right up. The ho'e could strut, and would work any strip I took her to. She was eager to get out there and make her pimp happy. Loved that about the ho'e.

There was no denying her ability to get out there and scoop the cream that makes the dream. But what was different about Daisy was how she saw things. The girl was weird, but weird in a positive way. The ho'e looked for the good in everything. Like when it was raining, I would be pissed cause wasn't no tricks on the strip and my money was low. That chick would say some shit like, 'well the rain is good for the farmers, and if they get a good crop we pay less for food, so it will all work out.' Now there was no way in hell me paying pennies less at

1

the grocery store was going to make up for a rainy day on the strip. But that's how Daisy thought, always looking for the positive. Wasn't a better bottom in The Chi.

Damn, a pimp is hungry. I could go for a Gyros sandwich and some fried mushrooms, but that little old white lady nurse wouldn't let me eat it anyway. A big pimp like me eats on the hour. I'm five eight, two hundred and sixty-eight pounds. I eat. And I come from people that eat.

My granddaddy was six foot three and three hundred thirty-five pounds when he died at eighty-nine. My daddy is six four and close to three-fifty. We big people and we eat. Eating a Gyros, a burger or something would probably knock some of the cold out of my spine. A pimp's teeth are chattering.

I might as well be out on frozen Lake Michigan, stripped naked and butt sliding across the ice, as cold as I am in this little mouse-hole room. And the blanket the old lady nurse gave me is thinner than the sheet. The blanket ain't doing a thing to warm me up. Every time I shiver it hurts from my toes to my nose. If I wasn't in so much pain, a pimp would get the fuck up out of here.

That little old white lady nurse must be pocketing my pain medicine and giving me dummy pills or something, because I'm hurting all over. She's going to have to give me two or three more blankets, and some more pain medicine. I'm keeping my finger on this button until she comes back.

This situation here ain't nothing nice. When I pull this thin blanket up my toes get cold, and if I leave it down my shoulders stay cold. I need another blanket. A pimp with four women is up here freezing like a homeless bum. I got two ho'es on the street, and two working square

2

jobs, and I can't get one of them to do a thing for me now.

I was pimping the two on the street hard, and macking the breath out of the two that work. Most thugs don't know the difference between a pimp and a mack, never mind trying to be both. My daddy is an old school gangster. He started his own gang thirty years ago, and still runs it. Hollis Jones been both pimp and mack, and I got most of my swagger from him.

When I was a little kid about eight years old he saw me beating up the boy who lived over us. I whipped the boy off his mountain bike and rode the bike up and down the block like it was mine. My daddy told me I was more boy than girl, and he started teaching me how to box.

He brought me up in the gangster life style he lives. Hollis Jones has never been broke, and I ain't never seen him not on top.

"Fuck asking. Take it. And if a clown got something to say, bust his motherfucking face," is what my daddy told me.

Living like that got me kicked out of school in the sixth grade. I decided early on that school and the whole square world wasn't for me. My daddy didn't make me go to school, and the state or nobody makes my daddy do a thing. He said as long as I could read, write and count money, fuck 'em.

Here comes the little old white lady nurse with pills and a little plastic shot glass of water. My eyes go to the clock on the powder blue wall. It reads eleven fifteen. Suddenly, I realize that I don't know if I been here days or hours.

"This is the last of what your doctor ordered, dear. After this we can't give you anything else."

"Damn, what you gave me ain't working," I say sitting up.

3

"I know it feels that way dear, but it is in your system. Nothing is going to alleviate the pain completely. Your nervous system is coming back to life. You are going to experience some discomfort."

Wiping sleep from my eyes, I ask her, "How long have I been here?"

"This is day three, dear."

A pimp couldn't have heard her right.

"Did you say three days?"

"Well, in forty-five minutes it will be four days, dear."

Three days. I couldn't afford to be laid up for three days. Major things are happening in my life, things that need my immediate attention, things that couldn't wait for three days. A pimp is dealing with situations that if I'm not careful could put me in jail, and leave me broke as a buster.

"Who been here to visit me?"

"The only visitors I know of, dear, are the federal agents outside your door."

She is smiling that adult smile. The one a grown person gives a cute little girl that has shitted her diaper and has her arms raised to be picked up. A person picks her up because she's pretty, even if she does smell like shit.

She steps behind me and begins propping up the pillows. She is surrounded by a flowery smell that makes me think about a funeral. That's creepy, a nurse that smells like a funeral.

"Has anybody called me?"

"The agents won't allow phone calls through to you, dear."

"How many of them are outside the door?"

"Two. It's always been two or more since you arrived."

4

I turn my head from her because her breath stanks. It reeks of peppermint, sardines and garlic. When my ability to move came back, my sense of smell came back, too, and it came back stronger than ever. A pimp can smell a fast flea fart. She walks from me to the raised television, cuts it on and leaves me alone in this closet of a hospital room.

With D.E.A. agents outside my door, and movement to my legs and arms just returning, leaving really ain't an option. The reality of this situation is . . . ain't a thing a pimp can do about life outside this room. The truth be told . . . everything has gotten out of my control anyway. Way too much is going on. I can't grab a hold of anything. Everything is falling apart. Even if a pimp could walk out of the door, I don't have the next move. And my daddy always tells me that, "when you don't have a next move, it's time to sit still and regroup." Since a pimp is stretched out and damn near locked down, this is the time to backtrack my steps.

Chapter Two

The first time a mack was in the hospital, I was thirteen years old. I had just finished finger fucking Babee Talbert, one of my square girls with good credit. I was sneaking out the basement window when her daddy mistakenly shot me. Of course once he saw who it was that he shot, he took me to the hospital.

When we got to the hospital I was not only bleeding from my shoulder, but from between my thighs as well. I thought the bullet had gone through my shoulder and came out of my cat. Being the young mack that I was, I passed out from fear.

Sure, I was expecting my period, and knew what it was. But for some reason when my menstrual happened, it freaked me out. Thank God for that kind-hearted Filipino nurse who calmed me down by better explaining the whole menstrual period thing to a thug. My daddy ain't never said the word menstrual as far as I know.

Days later, Babee's daddy came over to our place and apologized to my daddy for shooting me. When I came home from the hospital, my daddy gave me a chrome nine millimeter, and taught me how to shoot.

"Next time, shoot back," is what he told me.

Babee was the first girl to eat me out and get my clit hard, and I been sprung on the tongue every since. A mack loves getting head. That really is the only sexual thing I like. Sex ain't a big trip for me. Counting money is my thing. Playing in a woman's mind is better than playing with her cat. I'd rather romance a chick than sex her.

I make them smile with flowers and a nice restaurant, and be support for them. I let them know that I am the pimp and the mack that they can depend on. That it's me that got they back. Being there for a woman is more important than eating her out. A pimp has never left a ho'e in jail over night, and I know every situation my women are dealing with because we talk. If something is bothering them, I'm there with a fix, from a boss giving them grief, to another pimp eyeballing her; I am the mack with the solution. Most of my attention goes upstairs to they mind. Not that I won't work a ho'e dry with a strap on, but sex is secondary.

Babee got me sprung a longtime ago on getting head, but for me personally licking that twat is out. I ain't never been into that. I make most of my broads cum with my fingers. And besides, the women I meet be all about pleasing me, seems like they cum from eating my cat. All except Billie. That broad likes a whipping. She cums when I slap her around. She likes me to talk real nasty about her, and beat her across the butt with my belt. That's what floats her boat.

I got into pimping by robbing this weak ass dude on my eighteenth birthday. My daddy had rented this club on Forty-third Street east of King Drive. He got me a D.J. and everything. As if I had a bunch of friends to invite over. All I ever hung with was the younger dudes in E.O.G.: Benny Moon, Tray Six, Tommy Locke, and Duran. We was all founders' kids, our daddies were the high chiefs of Emperors of Game.

Even though I didn't invite anybody to the party, Duran and the rest of the clique had told people about it, so we had a nice little crowd with a couple of strippers dancing. I had on a pair of red and black checkered tailor-made pants, and a handmade black silk Chinese collared shirt, with a pair of red alligator men's shoes. My daddy had brought me the shoes for my birthday. He knows I love me some 'gators.

Well, somehow this pimp showed up with Daisy in tow. And as

7

soon as she walked through the door, my eyes were glued to her. As things worked out, she and the pimp sat at the table with me and Duran. I found myself staring at her despite the naked stripers on the crowded dance floor. She held my attention through most of the party.

I guess the curly-headed pimp saw me staring at her, because he said something about his ho'es not dating "stud broads." Hell, I know I'm stud, but it was the way the word sounded coming out of his mouth that pissed me off.

He sounded like my big-tittied, horse-toothed, third grade teacher who called me a dyke, and made me sit in the back of the classroom by myself, away from the boys *and* the girls.

He sounded like the little girl's mama who told her that as long as she was Black, she was never to bring a dyke home from school to play with.

He sounded like the doctor who told me not to come to his office dressed like a dyke, because I wore basketball shorts and Fruit of the Loom briefs to my first Pap smear exam.

But what really got to me, he made me remember curly-headed Teddy Miller, the boy I kneed in the balls who tried to kiss me when I was twelve. While crying from the pain of my knee in his balls, he whimpered out "dyke" as I stood over him laughing.

I heard all of them old voices through that pimp's mouth, so a thug like me jumped up and started pistol whipping him right there at the table. 'Stud' sounded like 'dyke' coming out of his mouth, and I hate the word dyke. So I whipped it out of his head.

I hate the word because I have never ever been able to find a definition for it, other than an offensive term for a lesbian. Which to me meant the only purpose of the word was to offend. The word came

8

to be because somebody wanted to piss a lesbian off. When I looked up nigger, at least it had reference to the color black. Bitch was a pregnant female dog, but dyke . . . an insult for a lesbian and nothing more. I hate the fucking word.

Once the pimp was out cold, I instinctively went through his pockets. The wimpy pimp had over five grand, Lexus truck keys, and a ounce of hydro. While Duran and them was hauling dude out of the back door, I looked over at Daisy, and the little black cutie pie said, "I was gonna choose you, anyway." And I had my first ho'e.

A thug had never thought about pimping. I knew my daddy had been a pimp, but I never actually saw him pimping. The pimps that I had seen I didn't like at all. I always thought of them as bloodsuckers, weak people who took advantage of weaker girls, silly girls with low self esteem, or girls looking for daddy substitutes, or somebody to tell them what to do and how to do it. I didn't understand a pimp's arrogance, or why pimps thought that they were entitled to money earned by someone else. But I didn't stay in the dark long about the money thing. It didn't take me a week to comprehend why a pimp is due the money earned by a ho'e.

Managing a ho'e is hard work: giving direction, balancing time, listening, reminding, and checking they thinking. That's a ho'e's biggest problem, her thinking. The job is trying to keep they mind right and on the quota. A ho'e will go in a rib joint and sit for two hours doing nothing if her pimp didn't focus her mind. I seen them standing on corners just watching cars pass by like they was counting the green ones or something. ho'es need they purpose told to them daily, through obtainable goals, quotas. A ho'e need to be told every day what is expected. And that is work.

When Duran got back to the table, he told me to keep the truck keys.

"Dude won't be needing 'em," he said and grabbed a naked stripper and danced onto the floor.

My daddy told me to work Daisy like a Hebrew slave, and to only give her half a day a week off. And the first day she brought me less than five hundred dollars, I was to beat her breathless.

All a thug like me knew about pimping was where the strips were. Back then I thought a pimp had to stay on the streets all night watching his ho'es. I was riding around in her old pimp's truck, so other pimps were staring at me hard. Young thug that I was, they staring didn't bother me. Yeah I was new to the strip, but not to the streets. I didn't know much about pimping, but I knew how to beat a jealous motherfucker's ass. I didn't expect any real trouble because them pimps knew about my daddy and my E.O.G. rank. They was jealous, not stupid.

Daisy brought me three hundred and fifty her first night out. I did like Hollis Jones said and drug her ass out of the Lexus truck and beat her right there on the strip for all to see. I left her on the corner bleeding out the mouth. Whipping her pretty ass wasn't an easy thing to do. But the game was and is the game.

The next night I parked the truck on the same corner. She got in with one thousand and seventy dollars and a ho'e in tow. The ho'e she had in tow, Billie, had five-hundred-fifty. At eighteen, I knew right then, that the pimp game was for me.

It wasn't until a week later did I go through the Lexus and find the five pounds of hydro. That put our clique into the weed game. Turns out that Daisy's pimp had six ho'es, but only she and Billie got on with me. I went over to the brownstone her old pimp had rented on Thirty-fifth and Giles, and kicked the other four ho'es out. Me and the clique made that brownstone a E.O.G. clubhouse.

Even though I was pimping, I was still down with the gang. I was still doing the robberies, home invasions, dope boy stickups, and still doing kidnappings. My goal was to get rich before I was twenty-one, so I worked every angle that came my way. I had fifteen grand in the legit bank and over fifty thousand in the safe in my daddy's basement. I figure a million in cash makes a pimp rich.

It was the dope boy stickups that got us deep into the crack rock game, which lead to the cocaine game, which lead to the D.E.A. agents outside my hospital room door. I really wasn't in the dope game deep. My women were paying me damn good. I did start selling rocks, but that was only because the chubby white girl that I was macking liked to smoke them. Her and her friends brought enough to get me in the game.

Macking, I was always able to get stuff out of females. It started in grammar school with butter cookies. I really, really loved them butter cookies, and most of the time a thug would just snatch a kid's cookie and eat it. I usually took a boy's. A thug didn't understand my liking girls back then, but I knew I didn't want to be mean to them.

One day this girl Brenda Paige sits next to me in the lunch room and gives me both of her butter cookies. She said she liked the peanut butter ones better, and then she asked me my name. I told her Dai Break Jones. Then she asked was I a boy or a girl. I told her I was a girl. Then she said that was too bad, because if I was a boy, I could be her boyfriend, and get her butter cookies all the time, because she liked my curly hair and my brown skin. She said her daddy was brown like me, and her mother was yellow like her, so because of them she said we would have been a good couple.

I liked the sound of that, 'boyfriend.' The thought of being her or any girl's boyfriend felt good in my ten year old head. My daddy was boyfriend to a lot of women. And as a boyfriend, he told the girlfriends what to do. It was girlfriends that came over and cleaned our house-- well apartment-- back then. It was a girlfriend that cooked for us, and washed our clothes, and went to the grocery store and brought back our food. It was a girlfriend who put cornrows in my hair when my daddy told her. Boyfriends had it made.

I told Brenda Paige I was a boy, and I was just tricking her when I said I was a girl, and that she could be my girlfriend and give me her cookies all the time. Because she was right, we would be a good couple. Then I kissed her right on the mouth in the lunchroom. That was my first mack move. And I been at it every since. The main part of macking is figuring out what a girl wants to hear, then saying it. I learned that early on.

The macking and pimping lessened my time with the Emperors of Game-- at least for a minute. A pimp got busy running ho'es from the Southside to the Westside, out to Evanston, and out to the truck stops in Gary, Indiana. My ho'es had got me running. Not to mention my square broads who I was taking to plays, out to eat, to the movies, to picnics, and to they family affairs. I didn't have time for nothing but my females.

Of course I heard it from my daddy and Duran, the thumb of our clique. I was one of five to a hand, and as one of five I had responsibilities to others. My daddy told me that if I couldn't pimp and handle my business with E.O.G., then I had to either share my pimp profits or stop pimping. I started handling my E.O.G. business a lot better. Pimping was a solitary thing. It required the thoughts of one individual. Only one boss was needed.

Duran wanted me around for the stick up jobs, which was what our clique did the best, and was the bread and butter for the other clique members and our soldiers. It didn't take me long to work out a routine that made Duran and my daddy happy. Once I-- as my daddy says-- got my priorities straight, doing both wasn't a problem.

With my girls, I was splitting all holidays, except Christmas, between Babee and Julia. I spent Christmas with Daddy. Just me, him, and lately, Cheryl. All day alone is how we like it.

Julia is my chubby redhead white girl from Downtown. A mack met her shopping at the Water Tower almost two years ago. I thought she thought she was flirting with a dude, until we went out that night. After dinner at the Cheese Cake Factory-- her suggestion-- we were sitting in my Chevy and I was rubbing on her thighs and playing with her ear lobes. I told her, "This thug is more man than any dude you been out with, but I was born female."

She didn't blink. She said she knew by my round hips and how my little titties curved up that I was female. She said fat men's titties sag down, but women's titties curve up. Then she flipped my Bears sweat shirt and went to sucking my little titties so good that my rusty knees started knocking. I wanted to buy the chubby redhead something when she finished . . . but game is game. What I told her instead was, "My Chevy needs a fill up."

She directed me to the gas station on La Salle and North Avenue. When I pulled into the station I told her to go pay for the gas and bring me an energy drink.

13

"Why should I pay for it?"

I expected the question and answered with, "Because I told you to." She twisted her face in protest. I added, "And because you can. You can help me a lot, and we both know it. And it's not just money either." My fingers went back under her skimpy linen skirt and on her thighs. "You know things I need to know about life. The way you ordered our dinner and how you talked to the waitress, you can teach me how to act in places like that. Smooth out my rough edges, show me what's what to this downtown world of yours." Then I popped out one of my titties and told her to come suck it, which she did with no hesitation.

I have been eating at downtown restaurants my whole life. A mack knows how to act in such places. Telling her that was game. Some people like to feel like they teaching you something, makes them feel superior. I saw right away that Julia was like that. She looked at me like an ignorant ghetto child who didn't know jack, one she needed to help. So I let her help me, a lot.

"You're not the first woman I have been with," she breathed out while sucking my tittie.

"I know. And by the way you put your mouth on me, I can't wait to see what else you can do with it."

She smiled when I said that, and hopped her chubby self out of the Chevy, and went and paid for the gas. And she been paying ever since.

Chapter Three

It was after my nineteenth birthday, and I had been in the pimp game about a year. It was only Daisy and Billie on the stroll, and I was still hanging pretty regular with the E.O.G. We all congregated at the brownstone on Giles. My square girl, Babee, was treating me like a king. The hydro was selling good, and word on the street was the young E.O.G. royalty and Dai Break Jones had it going on.

We all knew Duran really was the thumb, the leader to our five, but people on the streets saw me out front. I was the one pimping, dressing flashy, wearing rings and things, and with the big E. O. G. diamond studded necklace around my neck. The streets knew my daddy started the organization, so naturally people thought I was running the young heads.

Not that I couldn't have ran it, but Duran thought more than any of us. He was the last one to pull a pistol, and was always planning. He came up with the jobs and the execution. He never presented a job without a plan. That's why he was the real boss. I was his first soldier, and Tommy Locke was the second. Duran kept us in the loot, and that kept us paying up to the founders. My daddy and the rest of the founders loved him. My daddy even called him son. I had an issue with that for a minute, but I got over it.

It was a Thursday, and I had gotten to the brownstone early to check on Daisy. She was kind of sick the night before, and I wanted to make sure she would be able to work that night. Thursday night was a big night for the North Avenue strip, and I didn't want to miss that money due to her being sick. A pimp was getting real accustomed to ho'e money and didn't want to miss a dime of it. My girls were earning

15

good on the strip; the Thursday before they brought in thirty-five hundred from North Avenue.

I was squatted on the only sitting furniture in the living room, the slumped-in-the-middle blue corduroy couch, when Duran walked into the brownstone. He dropped a manila folder on the beat up and scratched wooden coffee table. The folder had 'Crap house job' written across the top.

We all sat on the raggedy couch, the carpet, or drug a chair in from the kitchen. The only thing we added to the clubhouse was the flat screen television that Tray Six's daddy gave us and had mounted on the wall. The bedrooms, bathrooms, and kitchen all had nice stuff in them just the living room was empty. But I wasn't spending a penny of my money on it.

When I looked at the folder on the table, I thought about the two crap houses on the Southside and the one out west that we went to. The one on the Westside was ran by Duran's daddy. The ones out south was owned by Benny Moon's daddy. Benny Moon was sitting on the swayback corduroy couch with me watching a Bear's game.

"Which one?"

Duran looked at me, and grinned his big gap-toothed smile when I asked the question.

Then he quickly walked by me, stirring up the air so that I smelled Daisy's cooking coming from the kitchen. She had a thing about always having fresh food on the stove every day. That afternoon the smell of mustard and turnip greens filled the clubhouse.

"Which one do ya think?" Duran sat next to Benny Moon on the sofa and put his left foot on top of his knee showing off his new orange and black Jordan's, which matched his orange and black Coogi jeans and top. The orange was going on, but I wouldn't have worn my new Jordans in all that snow. It was about three inches on the ground.

I had on an orange and brown walking suit myself, with some tan Timberland boots. We were always in competition with each other as far as clothes were concerned. Duran was always trying to out dress me, but he couldn't.

"We can't rob none of the ones that come to my mind, so I don't know."

People talked about Duran's skin because it was pitted and rough, and it had been that way since we was kids. He got into hundreds of fights over his skin, and I don't remember him losing one. Duran is tall, like six-three or something, and has a hell of a reach. He can knock a thug in the jaw from across the street. He gets his bad skin from his Columbian mama.

His daddy, Founder Aims, was robbing a jewelry store on Wabash and his mama was the manager or owner. His daddy kidnapped her because she wouldn't open the safe. His plan was to take her back later after he'd scared her half to death, but he never took her back to the store. Three weeks after he kidnapped her, they got married.

"Benny Moon?" Duran put his attention on Benny who was watching the game.

Benny Moon is a true Bears fan with season tickets. He answered, "Man, I'm down for whatever. Don't make me a difference. I'm two grand short on a Cadi. Ain't nothing safe right now. We can get any of them." He didn't take his eyes from the fifty inch plasma.

Duran laughed out loud. "Man, when y'all gonna start realizing our daddies ain't the only crooks in this city? There are crap houses in this city that ain't associated with E. O. G. Damn, it might feel like we own the world, but we don't. The city is bigger than us.

"A week ago, this honey from Roseland took me to a game out in the hundreds. A nice little spot. They roll on billiard tables, six games going on, and all the tables be full. I counted about fifty grand just at my table. This should be a quick, clean, fat-paying job. We got to move fast though, before somebody else gets them, they only been open a month."

The front bedroom door opened. Billie and fat-ass Tommy Locke came out, and she was naked.

"Ho'e, put some motherfuckin' clothes on. Ain't no free peep shows for these broke busters, and Tommy Locke better had paid your ass."

She walked a fifty over to me at the couch, and went back into the bedroom for her clothes. She was trying to entice Duran, because he was the only one who hadn't tricked with her, but he didn't want her or any prostitute. He thought paying for sex was a sign of weakness.

"We gonna go over everything tonight when it's just us here." Duran scoops the folder up and heads for the front door. "Y'all be back here at seven-thirty sharp; we move on this tomorrow." He never talked about work when my girls were around, and I didn't blame him, because ho'es talk. "Be sure to get Tray Six book-writing ass over here. We gonna need the whole crew for this. See y'all later." He zipped up his white, three-quarter length rabbit coat, and left.

Tommy Locke looked at me with questioning eyes, and dropped his fat butt on the couch, in the spot that Duran left empty. His weight added to mine, and caused the couch to sink even further down.

"We got work." I told him.

He grinned, because he loved to work. Tommy Locke was our pop-off man. He was usually the first in and the first to pull a pistol. Shooting a fool wasn't a thing to him. He was the one we had to control.

Benny Moon turned his narrow, half-Indian face from the fifty-inch and said, "'Bout time, cause I need me some money. Saw a Cadi on that lot on Western last night. Gots to get it." Benny Moon is almost the opposite of Tommy Locke. The only time he would gangster some shit was when we were all together.

"Let's just go *get* the Cadi. We done took rides from that lot before," was my suggestion.

He didn't move his eyes from the television to answer, "No, no, this one here is for my mama. She can't be riding around in no striker-plate ride. She got to have all the papers, legit all the way."

These thugs and they mamas, each one of them would walk through hell in gasoline draws for they mama.

Mine died the day after I was born. My daddy said it was because she was a punk to heroin. He made her stay clean while she was pregnant with me, but soon as I was born he said she left the hospital and ran out and got high. She overdosed at a spot on Thirty-ninth Street. People have told me that my daddy killed everybody in the place, chopped them up with a hatchet, and burned the place to the ground. They say he loved her like that. I have only seen one picture of her, tall, skinny and blue-black. Darker than me and daddy, and she was pretty. I never knew her. So a pimp like me don't miss her.

The closest thing I got to a mother is Benny Moon's mama. She is a Seminole Indian, and the only grown lady that was nice to me that wasn't fucking my daddy.

"What makes you think your mama will drive around in a Cadillac, anyway? You know she ain't all flashy." She was anything but flashy, spent most of her days in jeans and cotton blouses.

He looked at me with his good eye, and his crooked eye went over to the door, "She'll like this one cause it's green, a real pretty green. When I saw it, it made me think about down south in Florida where she's from. It's green like that; she will like this one." His pony tail flipped over his shoulder as he put his attention back on the game.

Benny Moon is one of my favorite people because he doesn't lie, and when he talks, he doesn't say useless shit. I like talking to him, so that day I tried to distract him from the game by saying, "You bet on the game or something?"

"Now you know I don't do that."

And I did. He watched for what he calls 'love of the game.' He will bet on anything else, except a Bears game-- and I mean *anything* else. Benny Moon loves to gamble. Too much is what I think, but nobody else thought it was a problem, so I stopped riding him about it.

Not that he ever listened to me anyway. He told me, "I'll stop gambling when you stop eating two Whoppers, a whole fried chicken, or a family size pizza by yourself. Everybody got something, Dai Break. You like to eat, I like to gamble. Tommy likes to smoke dope and to eat, Duran drinks, and Tray Six gambles like me. Everybody got something."

And for the most part, I believe that, except for my daddy. He doesn't drink, get high or gamble. Duran said my daddy's only weakness is spoiling me.

Tommy Locke pulled out a blunt, and struck it up with a wooden match. That was my signal to leave the area, because I can't stand smoke: weed smoke, cigarette smoke, incense smoke, crack smoke, none of it. Tommy Locke loved it all, weed smoke, cigarette smoke, hash smoke, and it turned out, crack smoke, too. And that's what got him fucked up.

E.O.G. law was strict about crack smoking. 'One to the head because you already dead.' And the law was being enforced. Five cats that I knew of had got they caps peeled, but none from our clique or our soldiers. Daisy told me Tommy Locke tried to pay her once with crack rocks. She said he had a pipe and tried to get her to take a hit. When I confronted him, he said Daisy was lying, and since she had only been with me a couple of weeks, I let it go.

I rose up from the couch and went into the kitchen where Daisy and Billie were. Daisy had on a long white T that hung to her knees, and was on the back of a pair of my old white K-Swiss. She was standing at the center island counter cutting up something, and Billie was sitting at the table in grey sweats and a black bra, painting her nails hot pink.

"Evanston is first tonight, ladies. I'ma take y'all out there about five. Pick you up about ten-thirty, and then head over to North Avenue. So pack a outfit to leave in the truck. How's your cold, Daisy?" I stood in the doorway talking, because I really wasn't planning on staying until five. I had a lunch date with Babee.

"It's fine, Daddy. I took the cold medicine you gave me last night, and I'm cutting up some chicken fat to boil down now. I'll be ready for tonight." She didn't look up from the chicken, and she sounded stuffed up.

"The weather man said it was going to be in the twenties tonight. Put together outfits that y'all can wear with coats, just in case. A sick

21

ho'e ain't shit to me. Come over here, Daisy." She looked a little wore out standing at the counter.

When she looked up from the chicken, I saw she wasn't alright. Her eyes were puffy and red and her nose was running. When she got to me, I touched her forehead. It was burning up.

"Damn! Yo' ass is sick. Go get in the motherfucking bed. Billie, finish up that chicken, and then go up to the corner and get a bottle of aspirin and a couple of bags of ice. We got to break her fever."

Not looking up from her fingernails, Billie said, "Daddy, I don't know what to do with that chicken."

I picked up Daisy and told Billie, "Bitch, boil it down and make soup. Shit, don't be ignorant your whole damn life."

I could feel the heat from Daisy through her white t. Instead of the bed, I carried her to the bathroom and drew a cold bath.

"Daddy, I don't want to get in that water. It's cold."

I don't know much about nothing, but I had seen enough television to know that when a person was as hot as she was, you put them on ice.

"Get in the fucking water and shut the fuck up. I can't stand a ho'e talking back, don't make me slap you."

I kept her in the tub until most of the two bags of ice melted. Made her take six aspirins, and put the ho'e to bed under a sheet. She wanted a blanket, but I couldn't risk her getting warm again. After an hour or so under the sheet, her temperature went down, so I gave her a blanket. Two hours later, with the whole pot of chicken soup in her, she was still normal, and didn't look that sick. I decided not to take her to Evanston. She would just work North Avenue, but Billie's ass was going to Evanston, and she was going to have to work her ass off to

22

cover my loss.

*

I got back from dropping Billie off at seven-thirty on the dot. The whole crew was at the brownstone, sitting at the kitchen table eating Daisy's greens and cornbread. I didn't think she had finished cooking the greens, but those hungry thugs didn't care. Anything she cooked, they ate. I had grabbed a Gyros and some fried mushrooms up in Evanston, and since it wasn't any room for me at the table, I took my sack up front and sat down on the couch.

Duran put the folder back on the coffee table, so I started flipping through it while I was eating. It looked like everything depended on speed. He wanted us in and out in less than four minutes.

"What do you think?" It was Duran asking. He was dragging in a kitchen chair.

"It looks tight, but you keep putting me and Tray Six out front when you know Tommy Locke wants in first."

"You and Tray ain't looking to shoot. Tommy is."

"Man, that ain't true." Tommy Locke came up front with a chair in tow. "I ain't popped a pistol in four jobs." He was followed by Tray Six.

"That's cause you haven't carried a pistol in four jobs. You carrying on this one."

"No shit!" Tommy Locke said, smiling like Duran had just given him an extra dick or something.

"We gonna all be strapped, but the only one that should have to pop off inside the place is Dai Break, and that's only to the ceiling and just to get people's attention. Tray Six, you on watch. If a thug moves after Dai Break pops off, you put one in his ass. The rest of us on table

23

wipe. You, too, Dai Break, after you shoot that first round off, you start wiping with Benny Moon. Tray, you stay on point, looking for a flinching thug. Tommy, me and you come through the door wiping tables, we not robbing the individual thugs, just the tables, in and out. On the way out, Tray, you backing out last. Before you leave, shoot out the lights and we up the stairs and gone."

"What about security?" I asked.

"They got two guards on the door. We get them soon as we roll up. Any thug flinch on the inside, Tray got 'em. Tonight, we gonna roll past the place, then later we go in two at a time so everybody can get familiar with the layout. It's in a basement, no real windows, just some little glass blocks. Any questions?"

From across the room we heard, "I think y'all need another person on watch with Tray Six; three people wiping is enough; you need eyes watching the people in the place." It was Daisy from the bedroom doorway. She was wrapped in the sheet and stumbling in our direction. "You need eyes on the people because gamblers be packing. One kid can't watch everybody. And you ain't leaving nobody to drive away. Who is in the getaway car?"

I was gonna stand up and smack the ho'e back in her place because her talking in a room full of men was wrong, and the ho'e knew that. But she collapsed in my arms and was red hot. The ho'e was burning up with fever.

I called my daddy, and he told me to take her to Provident's emergency room, and ask for Dr. Silverman. My daddy was to meet us there.

*

As soon as the nurses took Daisy's temperature they took her away.

24

My daddy came up to the hospital in his floor length black mink and gave me two grand for Dr. Silverman. I had loot, but I took the money anyway. The doctor told us she had walking pneumonia, and would be hospitalized for at least two days. He looked to my daddy who looked to me. I handed the doctor the two grand, and we left without filling out a form.

Chapter Four

What was funny about the whole thing was that Duran listened to Daisy's feverish advice. He put Tommy Locke and Tray Six on point and watch, while me and him were to wipe the tables. And he put Benny Moon in the stolen van as a getaway driver. We never had a getaway driver before. We always got in the car and fumbled with the damn keys, but even with a getaway driver the job didn't go right.

When we pulled up that Friday night, it was four guards not two, two in front of the door and two on the steps going down. The only thing we had going in our favor was the blizzard. The snow was so thick we could barely see them, and they couldn't see us.

My .9mm had the potato silencer, so I was to get the two guards, which I did getting out of the stolen van, popped them right off, but after I hit them, two more guards came up from the stairs with pistols blazing. I got hit in the thigh, and them two other guards had no silencers, so motherfuckers in the crap house had to have heard the shots.

I was thinking abort, but Tommy Locke let go of his two three-fifty-sevens and dropped both guards. Then Duran screamed, "Fuck it," and ran down the snow covered stairs. We followed him. Tommy Locke shot open the door and kicked it in. We all went into the big room popping off pistols. The gamblers inside the crap house hit the floor without us saying a word. Tommy and Tray went on watch while me and Duran got to wiping the tables.

I saw a thug sliding his bankroll into his sock. I kicked him in the balls and snatched the roll. Me and Duran wiped the last table together then hit the stairs. Behind us we heard Tommy Locke's three-fifty-sevens barking, but by time we got to the van we was all piling in as Benny Moon floored it.

"Four minutes and three seconds," Duran informed us.

It seemed like four fucking hours to me. I looked down at my thigh and the wound looked more like a rip than a gunshot. It could have happened jumping a fence. No doctor. Only some peroxide and some gauze was needed.

On the Dan Ryan expressway, we were headed north through the blizzard. Duran flipped open his cell phone, "Hey, baby, any police roll up . . . none . . . and only a few people left the spot so far . . . you think they still in there gambling . . . a black SUV carried away the injured dudes . . . you counted five, and no police yet . . . alright, baby, see ya tomorrow night.

"Looks like we clean y'all, no po-pos and them thugs went back to gambling. Where did you hit the guards, Dai Break?"

"I got both of 'em in arms like you said. I put them down, but not dead."

"Tommy?"

"Arms, man, no head shots."

"Cool. Them tables was loaded, we did good. Wait and see."

We dumped the van in Greek Town instead of in the 'hood. The further away from us the better. Then we caught cabs to Boy's Town where the truck was parked with our coats. A thug was cold as hell in that black hoody.

While I was driving south, just to fuck with him, I asked Duran was he cutting out a share for Daisy since it was her plan that we used.

The truck got quiet as we all watched him thinking. He was the original planner, but it was my girl's plan that we used.

27

He said, "Fuck that, man, I can't give that ho'e a crumb. You can give her a cut of yours, if you want."

The clique's eyes and ears went from Duran to me.

"Yeah right," I answered, "that ain't gonna happen. I'm mad 'cause she is in the hospital and ain't out there getting my money. She ain't getting a kernel from me. Besides, as sick as she was, she ain't going to remember having the plan."

Duran laughed and nodded his long head up and down. "You right 'bout that. She won't remember a thing."

He rolls the passenger window down and spits onto Halsted Street. Snow blows all through the truck, then everybody lets they windows down and the blizzard is in the Lexus. I rolled up all the widows and locked them.

"I'll cut her in," Benny Moon said.

"Me, too," Tommy Locke followed, "the ho'e alright with me. She always do right by me, cook for thugs every damn day, hell yeah, she get a cut. It's only right." Tommy Locke was dumping spent shells from the three-fifty-seven into his gloved hand.

Hearing them saying that surprised me. These thugs was talking about giving my ho'e money. I wasn't sure where it was going, so I shut up and listened.

"She was sick as hell and saw the holes in my plan. Imagine what the ho'e can think of when she ain't sick," Duran said, sounding serious.

"You saying you gonna cut her out a share?" was my question.

"I ain't saying that, because me cutting her a share ain't gonna do shit but swell your pockets. I'm just saying the ho'e got a brain."

"And the ho'e can cook real good," Tommy Locke added.

28

"What about you, Tray?" I asked while stopped at the light on Chicago Avenue and Halsted, by the Tribune truck docks.

"Shit, I'm with D-D-D-Duran. I'm not for putting mo-mo-mo-more cash in your pocket. We all took the same ri-ri-ri-risk. Why should we cut the ho'e a share for you to ta-ta-ta-take? I think we sh-sh-sh-should all chip in and buy the ho'e some jewelry or something. You wouldn't take th-th-th-that would you?"

Them thugs was tripping, "Man, fuck y'all! When y'all start caring about what I do with my girls?" I pushed down on the gas harder than I intended to, and all our heads snapped back as the truck went into a tail spin. I turned the wheels in the direction of the slide until I felt the tires take hold, then I straighten the truck out.

"Handle that shit, Dai Break!" came from Tommy Locke.

"I give a fuck about your ho'es, we talking about Daisy." I heard Bennie Moon pull the seat belt across himself and fasten it.

"Daisy is my ho'e. You thugs getting soft through your stomachs."

I eased up off the gas because two in the morning ain't the time to be going fifty-three miles an hour on Halsted with a truck full of just fired pistols.

"I know she a ho'e. I'm just saying . . . she a little bit mo'," Bennie Moon claimed.

"Yeah, she a cook," came from Tommy.

"She do my laundry," Duran offered.

"She edited the first three ch-ch-ch-chapters of my book," stuttered Tray Six.

"She took my grandmama to that dude that got her some cheap teeth, and she helped her fill out her Medicare papers," Duran said. "She do a bunch a shit, Dai Break, besides get your money." He was looking at me, waiting for a reply.

"Well, you know what? You thugs go on and buy her a piece of jewelry. You ain't got to worry about me taking it since she mo' to y'all. So I guess this means y'all ain't paying her to suck your dicks no more, since she mo' now?"

"I ain't tricked off with her in a minute," Benny Moon declared.

"Me n-n-n-neither. It just don't seem right no more. It's li-li-li-like having your crack head auntie suck your d-d-d-dick for a bag."

"Damn, you only gave your auntie a bag. I gave her two and got the pussy."

"F-f-f-fuck you, Tommy."

Duran stretched his arms behind him and sighed, "You know I ain't never tricked with Daisy."

If it wasn't Duran saying it I wouldn't have believed it. The rest of them started tricking with her day one.

"That's cause yo' ass is a cheap motherfucker," Tommy Locke added, "didn't want to pay the price, just like now. You know damn well you should cut her in a fair share."

Duran always goes with majority rule, and I guessed since I brought it up he counted my vote with Tommy, Tray Six, and Benny Moon, because he said, "Fuck it, alright. We will split into six and buy her something fly with her share. Now, that's it. I ain't trying to hear shit else about it." He always ends with 'I ain't hearing shit else about it' when the majority goes against his first wishes.

*

When we get to the brownstone we dump both bags on the kitchen table. It wasn't fifty grand on each pool table. The total take was only thirty eight thousand. Which got us six thousand three hundred and some change. Tray Six took Daisy's share and was assigned to get a nice piece of jewelry. That's one thing about our clique: what is said is done. Yeah, every thug in that room wanted to say fuck giving Daisy a share, after we saw the take, but what was said we did. After kicking up to my daddy and them, we each got fifty-three hundred dollars, which wasn't bad for a nights work.

*

When I got up to the hospital, I remembered I didn't know what room Daisy was in. Then the guard in the E.R. started giving me static about visiting hours being over, but all the while he was talking, his gaze was stuck on my diamond studded E.O.G. medallion.

I asked him, "How much for a security escort to the room for five minutes, and then right back here."

The guard looked up from my chain and passed his eyes up and down my red fox jacket and said, "a hundred and fifty dollars," with no hesitation.

Daisy was wide awake when I walked in.

"Daddy! I knew you was coming up here to see me."

She was in a private room with a view of the park.

"I would kiss you, but I don't want to catch whatever you got. How you feel?" Standing at the foot of her bed, I saw they had her on I.V.

"I'm ok, Daddy. Did you eat you some of the greens?"

"Nope, them thugs tore into that pot right after we left."

"Well, at least it didn't go to waste."

"They gonna buy you something, too."

"Who, Daddy?"

"The clique. They going get you something for thinking up the plan."

"What plan, Daddy?"

"Never mind. Your fever gone?"

"Feels like it, but my chest is so heavy and I'm spitting up the greenest, nastiest looking mess."

"Ok, ok, I don't need to hear any more. Miss you, baby." And I blew her a kiss. "When you get out we going down to the Ruth Chris and get you a steak, just me and you," I gave her a wink and blew her another kiss.

"Bye bye, Daddy."

"See ya later, baby."

When I got back to the truck it was five in the morning. The snow had stopped, but it was deeper than my boots and almost up to my calf. It was time to go scoop up Billie from Cicero Avenue. I had dropped her off south of Midway airport because she did damn good out there last week. She came up pretty good on North Avenue the night before, too. Wasn't no lying about it, the ho'e had been working her ass off.

When I pulled into the White Castle lot I saw her sitting at a table sucking on a straw. She was probably drinking a vanilla shake. Her and Daisy's favorite. She came out to the parking lot smiling. When she got into the truck she opened up her leather trench coat and pulled a nice sized fold from her black bustier, and counted off ten crisp one-hundred dollar bills, "I only had one date all night Daddy."

"What did you have to do, kill his wife or something?"

"Nope, he was a older guy. A diabetic. He said his 'wee wee' hadn't been hard in eight years. Not since his wife died. The deal was if I got him hard he would give me a hundred, if he stayed hard and came I would get a bonus. I been at that man's house all night Daddy, kept him hard most of the night and he came twice. He gave me five hundred for the work, is what he said, and the other five hundred was for the company. We watched movies and played backgammon, and talked, and all the while I was rubbing and kissing on his little wee wee."

The way she said wee wee made me laugh.

"That's my bitch! Tell me this: did he have the cash in the house with him?"

"Yeah, Daddy he had a little safe. He's a eye doctor with a office in the front part of his house. He gave me an eye exam and everything, told me my sugar was getting high."

"You remember where the house was?"

"I got his card, Daddy." She handed me the doctor's business card. "Did I do good?"

"You did damn good for a stupid stinking bitch like you is. When we get back to the clubhouse I'ma beat your funky low-life ass, like the slut your daddy told you you was. Now sit over there and play with your cat until we get home. And you better nut before we get there, bitch!"

A motherfucker woulda thought I had just given the ho'e some roses, by the grin that was on her face. Mean, nasty words turned her ass on. She let her seat back and went to work on herself because her pimp told her too. And since she did good, and I knew she liked dirty talk, I piled it on.

"Make some noise, you stinking ho'e. Let me know if it feels good. Get that cat soggy wet, bitch. Get it so wet I hear it smacking. Yeah, pull that pearl tongue, bitch, pull it!"

She was going at it so damn good, I pulled the truck over to watch.

"Yeah, bitch. I hear it now. That motherfucker is sloppy wet. Keep at it, bitch. Open them legs wider, wider, ho'e. Oh shit, yeah.

33

You getting my clit hard. Play with it, bitch."

By the time I got her back to the clubhouse, she had nutted so much, the ho'e was sleepy. She stretched out across her bed and passed the fuck out. It was seven in the morning. Babee didn't leave for work until ten. I wanted my cat ate and clit sucked. We missed our lunch date, so I knew she wanted to see me. It wouldn't be a problem stopping by. I had the keys to her place every since she moved out of her daddy's house.

Babee had bought one of them condo's on south Drexel. Parking was usually a pain in the ass over there, but I lucked out because squares was leaving for they day jobs. The elevator was down and I swear I didn't want to walk my big ass up two flights of stairs.

The steps were almost enough to change my mind, until I thought about how talented she was on the head tip. She's been making my knees knock since I was thirteen years old. I climbed the stairs.

As soon as I walked into her condo her gray tomcat jumps in my arms. This thug ass feline loves me fo' real. I got his ass out of the garbage can when he was a kitten and gave him to her. His ass been grateful every since. He ain't friendly with nobody but me and her. He still got his claws because I wouldn't let her neuter or declaw him. He be fucking her guests up, swiping they ankles when they sit down, and he be humping every girl cat that crosses his path. Maxy ain't no punk. I scratched behind his ears and rubbed his stomach. When I put him down he ran his ass over to the window and meowed, so I opened it and he jetted straight out. That was my thug for real.

I should have showered, but all I did was wash my cat and booty hole. When I walked into the bedroom it was two bodies in her bed and both was sleeping and snoring. The dude was her high-yellow

34

supervisor from her job. I knew she was dating the dude. She likes dick every now and then and I don't trip about it. It was just that I wanted to see her, so dude had a problem.

I go back into the bathroom and get my .9mm. I went over to him and shoved the tip up his nose, hard, and woke his punk ass up. He tried to say something but I smashed the butt of the .9mm into his eye. Yellow motherfucker got the message real smooth like. He got up, got his shit and hit the door. Dude still had the rubber stuck to his dick while he was getting dressed.

Babee snored through it all. I went over to her and kissed her lips, then her ear, and then I bit her nipple. She woke up and started looking around for dude. I didn't say shit, just propped up a pillow and opened my legs. She gave me what I came for, and gave it to me good.

When I ain't nutted in a while I squirt. I usually let her pull away from the squirt, but I held her head in place and drenched her face. When she looked up, she was a glazed motherfucking doughnut, and I pushed her head right back down there. And she went to work again.

I didn't squirt the second time, but I let loose a good one. And she kept sucking my clit after I let go the second big one and gave me a couple of more little ones. The shit was so good I started crying her name, she came up to me and we kissed for a long time. Then a thug like me . . . fell asleep.

When I woke up it was eleven thirty in the afternoon. Babee was there laid on my tittie, and Maxy was perched atop her wicker love seat by the window. Her wooden blinds were open and slits of sun shone through the horizontal slices. Babee shouldn't have been there; she worked on Saturdays.

"Why you didn't go to work?" I started playing with the brown twist at the top of her head.

"I didn't want to see Chester. I didn't know what to tell him."

"Why you got to have something to tell him?"

"He's my boss, Dai Break. I work for him."

"So?"

She sat up pulling her twist away from my fingers and her head off my tittie.

"So? You came over and probably threw him out. I got to tell him something, and besides, we went to the boat last night and I . . . I messed up my mortgage money, and he was going to give it to me this morning."

"He was gonna pay your mortgage for some cat?" I looked up at the maroon ceiling, not at her. It irritates her if I talk to her and don't look at her, and not looking at her also lets her know that what we are talking about is bugging me.

"I just didn't want to go to the bank, and at the time it seemed like a good idea."

I didn't say a word because sometimes when you macking a bitch you got to remind them that you have all the solutions. I rolled out of the bed and went into the bathroom and peeled seventeen hundred dollars from the crap house loot. I placed the money on her thigh. "You ain't got to ho'e. Damn, girl. You with Dai Break Jones. You know better."

I went back into bathroom, showered and left without saying shit else.

Macking and pimping is different as night and day. If I was pimping her, we would have called that yellow dude back and got that cash, but as her mack, she needs to know I got what she needs. Besides, I know for a fact that she has over forty grand in the bank. The seventeen-hundred dollars wasn't shit but a gesture, a mack move.

Chapter Five

I was going home to eat lunch with my daddy and sleep in my own bed, but soon as I got in the truck, Julia started blowing up my cell. I would have ignored her calls, but I hadn't spent time with her in a couple of days, so I answered, "Hey, Sugar Girl," my pet name for her.

"Hey, Danny. I'm here with Bret and some friends and they need you know what."

"Oh, yeah?"

"Both. They want to chop some trees and roll some rocks."

They wanted weed and crack. "What they looking for?"

"They need a pound sledge hammer to help with the tree chopping, and they are behind the eight ball three times for rock rolling."

"Cool, I'll be there in less than an hour."

They wanted a pound of weed and three eight-balls of rock cocaine. Julia thought she was talking in some ghetto dope dealer's code that would trick the police. I told her if the police were listening in to her phone or mine, we were already fucked, and talking in code wouldn't help.

I had to go back by the clubhouse to fill the order. The clique has been in the weed game since we found that hydro in back of the pimp's truck. We sold that, and started copping from Benny Moon's daddy on the regular because it was good money in weed. Between the five of us we moved about ten to twelve pounds a week. The profit is between fifteen hundred and two grand. We try to sell it in half pounds and pounds.

We got into the crack game after we kidnapped this thug who disrespected Tommy Locke at the barbershop. An older dude about

38

thirty-five. Gene Taper was his name. Tommy Locke was next for the chair and Gene walked straight in the shop and took the seat. They exchanged words, and Gene didn't move from the barber's chair. He told Tommy Locke to go fuck himself, and since he was bald he could go get a disposable razor and shave his own damn head. He told Tommy Locke it didn't make sense for him to take up space at the barber shop since he was a "baldheaded motherfucker."

People in the shop laughed on the side of Gene. Tommy laughed, too, sat around for a couple of minutes then left the shop.

When he got outside he called us over. It was cold as polar bear farts that day. We were all in fox jackets that Tray Six's daddy had got for us. It was funny because we didn't know that each other was wearing the coats. When Tommy called us to him we all rolled up in the foxes. He wanted us to go in and beat everybody's ass in the barbershop who laughed at him, while he shot Gene Taper in the head.

Fortunately, Duran came up with a better plan while we were standing on the corner in the freezing wind. Gene Taper was the big dope man in that area, and got most of his product from Benny Moon's daddy. Killing him would lessen E.O.G. profits, and that was a violation even founder's kids couldn't afford. What we could do, if we kept it to ourselves, was kidnap Gene and hold him for ransom. When he said keep it to ourselves, we all looked over at Tommy Locke because he was known to talk like a chick. He responded with, "Fuck all of y'all. I ain't gonna say shit."

Duran flipped up the collar on his fox jacket against the wind and told Tommy Locke that Gene couldn't even know that it was us that got him. Tommy Locke said fine, and we got our asses off that cold corner.

Tray Six was assigned to follow Gene Taper the first day. The second day it was me. The third was supposed to be Benny Moon, but Duran decided to grab him the third day. After we saw that he went to ten o'clock mass two days in a row, we got him coming out of mass on day three. We didn't have him for four hours. Duran asked for fifty grand and three birds. His wife dropped off thirty grand and two kilos to the Locker at Bleeker's bowling alley, with a note saying that was all that was in the safe. When we called Duran with the information he called the motel manager of the Do Drop Inn and told him a man was tied up and gagged in room thirty-three. We had rented the room using Gene Taper's identification and credit card. And that got our clique into the crack game.

All of us except Tray Six had sold weed and rocks before independently. His daddy tried to keep him away from street game, and was always sending him away to school, but Tray would run away from the school and come back to the city. When he turned sixteen his daddy gave up on shipping him off, but made him get a high-school diploma. His daddy told him that if he didn't graduate from high-school he would shoot him in the knee and give him a limp. Tray Six believed him and graduated. He didn't know much about selling drugs, but he knew about hiding them.

He had cut and glued together some of the floor boards in the kitchen; he glued them in such a way that we could lift them up and stash the kilos under them. The weed he put behind the plaster boards in the closets. He turned the back walls into swinging doors. They look like the back of the closet until the base board and top are pushed at the same time, and the wall opens like a door.

I was in the closet in Billie's room pulling out a pound when she

40

woke up.

"Is that you, Daddy?"

"Yep."

"When is Daisy gettin' out?"

"I think tomorrow or the next day."

I closed the phony wall back and stepped out of the closet with a pound and a half of weed.

"Will you take me up to the hospital to see her before I go to work tonight?"

It was going to be Saturday night. Broadway and the truck stops out in Gary would be the strips she worked. I decided right then not to have her work the truck stops by herself, because if a trucker snatched her, which had been known to happen, both of my ho'es would be off the streets. And a pimp couldn't have that.

"Yeah, I'll take you up there. You just working Broadway tonight, no Indiana."

With the closet light out, the afternoon sun was the only light in the bedroom, and the beams passed through the window and landed on Billie's half-sheet covered body. She was laid on her stomach with one ass cheek exposed. She hadn't turned her head on the pillow to face me while she talked.

She'd cut her hair very short, almost to the scalp, and dyed it blond, along with her eyebrows and cat hair. I liked the contrast with her cocoa-colored skin. It made a trick pause to look at her. Billie liked boys more than girls. She liked the rough stuff and group sex, dicks up her ass and cat and shoved down her throat all at the same time. She liked being the only female with three and four guys. Dumb bitch, but

41

to each they own. Them parties made money though. Tricks have paid me up to seven hundred to get her on a group sex date.

I'd promised her a butt whipping the night before, and a pimp looked at that plumb ass of hers and thought about doing it right then. Billie had a big ole ass and wide hips and I kind of liked working her with the strap-on doggy style because she said crazy sexual shit while I was riding that big ass of hers. I put the strap on in her cat and a vibrator in her booty hole. Billie gets possessed after ten minutes of it, and gets to speaking in some crazy ass language. I had gotten myself kind of worked up thinking about it, but money was on the schedule so I smacked her hard on the naked ass cheek she had exposed.

I told her, "I ain't forgot about how you came up last night, you stankin' ass ho'e, you fell asleep on me bitch, but I'ma tear that funky cat up when I get back so have your trifling ass ready."

*

Julia had me come to her parents' house in Lincoln Park. They had left for France that morning. "To enjoy the winter season," was how Julia said it. They weren't coming back until Thanksgiving week, so Julia was floating on the freedom. She answered the door in her jeans, and white cotton blouse which was unbuttoned to her navel.

We walked straight through the townhouse to the white wood paneled recreation room where Bret and two skinny brunettes were stretched out on the gray leather couch and easy chair. Bret was in the chair. I had done business with him in the past. He was always eager to get the dope, and never haggled over price. The white boy with jet black hair was just happy to find somebody with the quality and quantity of dope he needed. I guess we had good drugs because no one ever complained.

42

I charged him two hundred more than the price our clique paid per pound, and fifty more than we charged people in the 'hood, per eight-ball. He didn't blink an eye in protest as he counted out my cash. Like before, Bret got his dope and left. The two brunettes, Madelyn and Pauline, were still there. I hadn't met either before.

Madelyn wanted an eight-ball and Julia wanted some crack and weed. I brought extra dope with me, because Julia always got the order wrong. She was so into talking in code, her ass forgot the amounts, and it happened all the time. I caught Madelyn looking hard at the crotch of my black sweat pants. I was still in the stick up clothes from the crap house, black sweats and pullover. I guess she was trying to figure out if I was guy or a girl.

"What you looking at, bitch?"

I caught the brunette off guard with the direct question. A thug stood over her and dropped the eight-ball of crack in her lap and extended my hand for the money. My crotch was in her face. She sat back on the couch and reached into her jeans and pulled out the money. She handed it all to me and got up off the couch and fled to the other side of the recreation room by the television.

Counting the money, I saw that she had handed me twenty dollars too much. I said nothing, and took the empty seat she left on the couch.

The other brunette looked at me and said, "I know you, but not as Danny. The people we both are acquainted with call you Dai Break. You drive a Lexus truck and wear a fifty thousand dollar diamond E.O.G. medallion around your neck." She wasn't scared about putting my background out there like that.

"That chain is real, Danny?" Julia asked.

43

"And how you know this?" I asked the ballsy brunette left on the couch, while ignoring Julia's silly ass question.

"Because I use to be with Popeye off of Cicero, and I saw you on the Westside and on North Avenue. People in the life talk about you, and I was at this year's Players Ball. You damn near won Rookie of the Year with only two ho'es. I think it was a good thing you didn't win. That would have took the hatin' to a whole different level."

The little white ho'e knew some shit, and she was talking like she was choosing a pimp. She said she use to be with Popeye, so she wasn't green to things. A pimp had seen that a white girl on the stroll was both money and trouble. Cops gave a pimp more static for having a white girl in the family, especially one as young as Pauline. The girl couldn't have been seventeen. I pulled my E.O.G. necklace from under my sweatshirt. It hung to my lap.

"Julia, when you start hanging with prostitutes?"

The question made her grin that kiddy smile of hers. The one she gives when she thinks she's up on me about something. The one that shows her dimples, and makes her green eyes sparkle, and turns her chubby cheeks almost as red as the hair on her head and her cat.

"I told you, you weren't my first, Danny. Pauline and I have been friends since Charter Barclay. That was the inpatient adolescent unit our parents sent us to. You see we go way back."

Yeah, she told me about her folks sending her to a crazy house for kids. I thought that was fucked up. But she didn't seem to mind much. Said they would send her once a year or so after she turned eleven and stopped talking to them, and started cutting herself, and crying in her room for hours at a time. When I asked her what was wrong she said, "Nothing, I just had some issues to work out."

44

Julia told me that once she started smoking weed and crack, and snorting heroin, she was able to stop taking the psychiatric medicine. I told her that didn't sound too smart, but she said it was. And I didn't say nothing else about it.

"Why you leave Popeye?" was my question to Pauline.

Yeah, she might of swollen my pockets with fresh ho'e money, but I wasn't in the mood to be beefing with a pimp from out West. I spent time over there and didn't need shit getting in the way of my money.

"Popeye's ho'es don't eat. I was living at a mission and making my five hundred dollar a night quota. I couldn't tell you the last time I slept in a real bed. He's living out of his Benz. I didn't get into the game to be a broke ho'e. The dope boys is pimping him. Popeye is smoking crack. I'm over here now because I couldn't stand another day in the mission. What sense does it make to be ho'ing all night, but sleeping in a day shelter or the bus station?"

If it was the truth, that was a fucked up way to live. No real pimp had his girls living in a shelter.

"Damn, bitch, that is some foul shit to say about your pimp. You must be looking for a new daddy?"

Like Peter Paul say, try 'em all. I looked the little white ho'e straight in her eyes, and she didn't lower them.

"Yes, I am."

The ho'e stood up and turned around in front of me. Wasn't much to her, a little ass, no hips and tiny ass titties, but her hair was long and she was sort of pretty, with them brown eyes and brown hair.

To make sure, I said, "You choosin', ho'e?"

"Yes, Dai Break, I'm choosing you. I want to be down with you."

Loved the sound of those words, a pimp almost gave up a smile, but I had to be in control because the truth of the matter was, the ho'e was desperate. Her pimp was a buster and she needed a real pimp to lead her ass from the poverty she was living in.

"Is that right? But I ain't got no white ho'es in my family. You'd have to really be qualified and *bona fide* to get on with me."

I looked over at the tall coo coo-clock in the corner. "It's what? Two o'clock? Empty your pockets on the table."

She puts about thirty dollars and some coins on the table.

"Okay, bitch, I'll give you until three thirty to come up with two hundred dollars. You do that shit in the daytime, up here in Lincoln Park, then I'll know your ass is qualified enough to be with the specialized. Get going, ho'e."

The little skinny white girl didn't hesitate to hit the door. The other brunette had opened her eight-ball and had got to smoking over there by the television. I doubt she heard a word of what we were talking about. I pulled out another eight-ball, split it in half for Julia. Put up my half, and split her half again.

"Half is for you, the other half is to sell. Okay? Don't smoke it all." I pulled out the half pound of weed and tossed it on the table, too. "Sell that, too. Break it down into quarter ounces. If anybody want's more, then call me."

She came over to me and sat on the floor at the coffee table.

"How much do you want back in total?"

"Give me four-fifty."

"Okay," she reached under the table for her purse and got the money.

"You should make about eight hundred if you do like I showed you last time."

46

"I remember. Tenths of a gram of rocks, and seven grams of weed is how I am to sell it."

I reached down and fuzzed up her red hair and kissed her on the back of the neck.

"So, what you gonna do with this whole house to yourself?"

"Have a couple of parties to sell this, then have you spend some early mornings with me. You and I alone should be very pleasing. Oh, and I want to go to a concert in Uptown next Thursday. Springsteen is coming. I got tickets for the concert and a hotel. Are we on?"

She loved to be seen with me, and I liked that about her.

"Hell, yeah, I think I can make that one. We can have another picnic in the hotel."

I said yeah, because it was kind of cool in Uptown. People were relaxed. White people, black people, black and white people together, gays, thugs, and stud broads with they chicks. Everybody was up there and nobody tripped about a thing. It was way relaxed, and I liked it.

"Good." She kissed my knee and winked up at me. "I had a great time at the last show."

"You gonna get some more of that goat cheese and wine?"

"If you like."

"And since we staying overnight, that means you in lingerie, right?"

"If you like."

"You know I like."

I reached into my back pocket and pulled out the bankroll I took from the dude that moved at the crap game stick up. Opening the roll, I saw it was three hundred and fifty bucks. I put the money on her thigh and said, "Get a couple, one baby doll one, and one fish net one for sure. And go past the adult book store and find us something to

47

play with."

She scooped up the bankroll and dropped it in her purse, "You didn't like the last toy I brought. You sure you trust me?"

Yeah, she tripped last time I sent her to the bookstore.

"Sugar Girl, you brought a two-headed dildo and you know the only thing I like in my cat is your tongue, so get whatever you think I will play with."

"Can I bring someone?"

"Who?"

She nodded her head towards the crack smoking brunette. I had almost forgot she was over there.

"Does she play like we play?"

"Not yet, but by Thursday she will."

Looking at the girl, I didn't think she was fifteen, but she smoked crack like a grown ass hype.

"Bring her if you want, but don't let her spoil our good time. Make sure you try her before the concert. If you want I'll come over and turn her fresh ass out this week."

Julia, who had just turned eighteen herself, was always surrounded by teenage girls. She liked to shock them with the bi-sexual thing.

"You have already taken Pauline. Now you want Madelyn, too. Aren't we selfish?"

I stretched and yawned while sitting on the couch.

"Pauline ain't a certainty. She got to pass the test."

"Do you test all your whores?"

"Now you know we don't talk about that? That world ain't for you."

"Pauline has told me some things, and if not for the fear of AIDS and the fear of being sodomized, and having to suck so many dicks, I might have gone out there for the experience. Tell me, will you make love to her if she becomes one of your whores?"

"That ain't your business, Sugar Girl."

"Will you beat her if she doesn't make your quota? Will you provide her housing? You know she has no place to lay her head. I was going to let her stay here until my parents returned. Her parents left the city two years ago for Virginia. She's all alone here, Danny. Will you feed and clothe her?"

I pulled off my black hoody and said, "Come up here and put one of these in your mouth." She quickly shot Madelyn a look, but didn't hesitate to join me up on the couch. Madelyn tried to act as if she wasn't watching, but I kept catching her glance.

I told Julia to pull off her jeans and ride my knee while I sat on the couch. She loved to do that while sucking my tittie. I had to take my sweat pants off because she would have soaked the material. We was both naked and little Ms. Madelyn was finding us hard not to watch. I sat gapped legged, and when I caught her eyes between my thighs I pulled the hood back on my clit. I heard her gasp. My clit is big enough to be seen from a across a room. Julia was going to town on my knee and about to bust a big ass nut. She let out a moan that made Madelyn drop her crack pipe.

I told her, "Come over here and let me stick my finger in your cat." Oh, she wanted to, bad, but instead of moving towards us, she picked up the pipe and put another piece of crack rock on it and lit it with her eyes still on us. Julia came big time and slid down to the floor. Me, I stretched out on the couch and kept my eyes on Madelyn until sleep took me.

49

Pauline woke me up with three-hundred-and-sixty dollars, all in twenties, tens, fives and ones. That meant the young ho'e went straight to work. It was four o'clock, but I gave her a pass because she was a young white girl and that was good money on black strips. I would have still snatched the young ho'e up had she come back with only a hundred dollars. I got dressed and told her, "Welcome to the family, bitch."

Daisy called me while I was walking out of Julia's house. She was getting released from the hospital and needed me to pick her up. I told her to give me an hour or so because Pauline needed some clothes bad. I could not have her meet Daisy or none of the clique looking as raggedy as she did.

*

The little ho'e started crying because I bought her a winter coat, a few new clothes, got her hair cut, nails done, and bought her a little pearl pinky ring.

"It's been a long time since I been in a store and bought some clothes or got myself groomed. I'm down with you, Dai Break Jones. You haven't made a mistake. I promise."

"We'll see, ho'e."

When we got to Provident Hospital, I sent Pauline in to get Daisy. I figured they could start getting to know each other, and besides I had some calls to make. The first one was to the number on the business card Billie got last night. It was answered on the second ring by a perky sounding office worker. Her answering told me the eye doctor was still in business.

The second call was to my daddy. We check in with each other daily, and since I missed lunch he was probably a little worried. He told

50

me he was on his way to the doctor because his new diabetes medicine had his bowels running. Tray Six's daddy was taking him there, but he wanted me to pick him up. He wanted to talk about Duran and his plans.

I hated talking E.O.G. business with my daddy, because I had no plans of taking it over. Fuck running a organization, that shit took too much from your life and didn't give enough back. I was down to E.O.G., but I didn't want to run it.

Duran and Tommy Locke was the only ones in our clique that planned on running E.O.G. in the future. Tray Six was writing a book and taking a writing class up at Chicago State. Benny Moon had bought a couple houses in Florida was and planning to get more. I really didn't know what I was going to do, but I knew I wasn't going to be pimping or thugging for life.

My daddy is counselor, preacher, teacher, advisor to over two hundred thugs and they families, and leader to over twenty five hundred soldiers. The closest two hundred call him for everything, any decision in they lives they involve him; from where to move, to what car to buy, to who they should marry. He has more godkids than the Pope. No way I wanted all that in my life. No fuckin' way. And my daddy knew it. He said I was running from the responsibility of my birthright.

Pauline and Daisy walked out of that hospital looking like new money. The contrast was striking. Daisy was black and shiny, like just-dressed tires, and Pauline was white as fresh snow, and by the smiles that was on both they faces, they was hitting it off pretty good. Daisy climbed into the front of the truck with a, "Hi, Daddy," and gave me a kiss on the cheek.

51

"I feel really good, and seeing Pauline made me feel even better, Daddy." She had on a different coat and clothes than the ones I brought her up there in. Ain't no telling who did what for her while she was at the hospital, since she is 'mo' to the clique. I noticed the new tennis bracelet, but didn't say a word.

"Will you take me to the grocery store, Daddy? I want to cook a good ole dinner for everybody," she said, looking down at the new bracelet and smiling. My daddy probably wanted to go to the store, too. I was about to say yeah when we was suddenly swarmed by police; a detective car and two blue and white squads.

They pulled us out the truck like boogers, and flicked us against the squad cars. A dude cop was patting me down, but once he got to my titties he stopped cold and yelled, "Female officer needed." He kept me pinned to the hood of the squad by the back of my neck.

I saw a uniformed officer pull my .9mm from under the seat, with the half of eight-ball. He looked at me and smiled. I thought I was fucked, until the officer looked behind him and then to his left, then he looked right at me and blew a pimp kiss. Then my pistol and the crack went into the crouch of his pants.

When a female officer came over, she said, "What?"

"It's a woman," the dude cop said about me and released my neck. But she immediately returned me to the same position and kicked my legs even wider apart. Women cops are worst, always trying to prove how hard they are. She put the cuffs on me tight enough to choke a damn worm.

They put Daisy and Pauline in the back of the same squad car. I was by myself. The police squads didn't move until a city tow truck came and hitched up to my Lexus truck and towed it away.

They un-cuffed us as soon as we got to Police Headquarters' on Thirty-fifth Street. These two detectives put us all in a meeting room and said we weren't under arrest, and apologized for the uniformed officers cuffing us. The two detectives that escorted us to the room were a strange pair. The one named Lee had long red dreadlocks and dressed like a hippy. The other one, Dixon, was balding and had bad breath and wore horribly cheap shoes and a cheaper suit. The man's breath was foul as a sewer. I had heard of both of them, but this was my first time meeting the homicide dicks.

It was all about the damn Lexus truck. The police found Daisy's old pimp's body in a burnt out building on Forty-third Street. It couldn't have been nothing but a skeleton after a year. It seems that Detective Lee ran his name through the DMV and matched the truck.

The streets talk to cops, especially crack heads and thugs with pending cases. They will give up they mamas, so I know he didn't have a problem finding out about the truck, or who was driving it. But me and Daisy had come up with a story just in case this happened.

"He left the truck with Daisy a year ago. He told her he was riding home with friends, and left her at my birthday party. We ain't seen the man since," is what I told detectives Lee and Dixon.

Daisy pretty much gave them the same answer I did, but she added, "Do I get to keep the truck?" And she was so damn sincere when she asked, I was expecting the cops to tell her yeah, but they told her no, and offered the three of us a ride to our destination. I refused for us. Being seen in police cars wasn't a good thing for me, or any E.O.G. member.

Dixon, the detective in the cheap suit, was standing in front of the door of the meeting room blocking our exit.

He looked at me and said, "I know who your daddy is. I know who you are. I know you think you a man, and I know you pimping." He looked at my girls and kept going with, "I know these are your ho'es and I know for a fact . . . that your crew stomped the owner of that truck to death. Now, what you need to know . . . is that I'ma find a way to pin this shit on you. You can't have a man stomped to death and drive around in his fucking truck for a year!" He sprinkled me with spit when he yelled. "Not in my gotdamn city. Dai Break Jones, I'm coming for you. Tell your daddy and all the rest of that E.O.G. slime . . . now you and your filthy ass ho'es get the fuck out of here."

He straight shocked me because I thought things were going pretty smooth up until then. The attack was out the blue, and I wanted my reply to be just as shocking to him. I wanted to say something real slick, but he hadn't threatened me with harm or disrespected me directly, and he did have the power to lock my ass up in jail overnight, so what I carefully said was, "Good luck with a year old corpse, and since you know so much . . . know this . . . I ain't scared of yo' ass, I heard about you, too . . . Mr. Limp Dick."

Judging by the way his eyes bucked, I had went too far. He grabbed me by the throat and laid me out on the meeting room table. The dreadlock detective sprang up from his chair and pulled him off me. I was only guessing he had a dick problem. I must of guessed right.

Walking out of Police Headquarters, the reality of how things could have gone settled around me. I could have caught a gun case and a drug charge had that uniformed officer not been a crook. I thanked the Lord for crooks.

54

Chapter Six

My daddy found the whole thing funny, even us picking him up in a cab made him laugh. But he didn't get in the cab. He called Duran for a ride and told Duran to drive him and Daisy to the grocery store, while me and Pauline were to take the cab to his house. It became apparent that we were all going to have dinner with my daddy.

"Told ya a year ago to dump dat damn truck," my daddy said out of the passenger window of Duran's '73 black Eldorado with the Super Fly chrome front. And he did. He told me more than once to get rid of the truck. I kept it because it was a free Lexus, and driving it got me a little more street credit. I saw Duran laughing as they pulled from the curb.

"A hard head makes a soft, so' ass," my daddy said, rolling up the window.

I didn't tell him about the pistol, because he told me to stop leaving it in the truck. 'A pistol in the truck can't shoot back for you,' is what he had said.

I walked back across the street to the yellow cab waiting in front of the store front building that held my daddy's doctor's office. I got in the cab and looked up at the meter; it was up to forty dollars from waiting on Duran. I gave him my daddy's address, knowing that was going to add another twenty dollars from the doctor's office on Taylor Street to daddy's place on Forestville.

I had a '68 Chevy Caprice in my daddy's garage, but I had got used to riding in late model luxury with the Lexus. Instead of going to daddy's house, I decided to make a stop at the bank, then call Mike Love and get me a car. Looking over at Pauline, I said, "Want to go car shopping with your pimp, ho'e?"

"Oh, yeah, Daddy, I would love to."

Mike Love had a serious thing for white women. If I worked it right, a pimp could get a couple grand knocked off of whatever vehicle he had that caught my eye. He did business by picking a customer up and taking them to wherever he had the cars stored that week. He never kept more than five vehicles and was constantly moving his inventory. He ran the business with his son. One of them would pick the would-be customer up and take them to the cars. I had the cab driver take us to the bank on Forty-seventh and Cottage Grove.

I withdrew ten grand from savings, and went back outside to join Pauline sitting on the bus stop bench. The evening sky was out. Some thug had pulled up on her and was trying to get her to get into the car for free. I stood next to her and she rose and gave me a kiss. Dude gave me the nod and drove off. I dialed Mike Love's number on my cell, and told him it was Dai Break Jones, and he said "No problem, what's your twenty?"

"Huh?"

"Where are you, Dai Break?"

"Oh, on Forty-seventh and Cottage Grove at the bus stop in front of the bank."

"I'm right around the corner, be there in a second."

Mike Love sells striker plate cars, stolen new cars with made up registration numbers on the strips of metal on the dash and door. He gives you phony registration papers and everything. The papers will get you past a traffic cop, if he doesn't run you through the computer. If the cop runs you through, the number comes up blank in the system, not stolen; usually the cop thinks something's wrong with the system and lets you go.

Mike Love and his son sell the cars for ten grand a pop and no refunds. He sells new Mercedes, BMWs, Ranges, Porsches, all the expensive ones. My daddy wouldn't buy one because of the no refund policy. But for me, being young and making money, it was worth the risk to get an eighty thousand dollar car for ten grand. Besides, a pimp like me had to flash.

Mike Love picked us up in a big white Cadillac Escalade, and drove us to a carwash on Ninety-first and Ashland. Squares / regular people was in the warehouse-looking carwash getting they vehicles washed, not knowing what else was going on around them. Parked in the back of the carwash was another pearl white Escalade, a Porsche truck, and a big BMW sedan, and a black Lexus truck. The Lexus was latest model, which was two years newer than the one the police took from me.

As I hoped, Mike Love's eyes hardly left Pauline's lean little body while he was telling me the features of the truck. I nodded my head towards him when I had Pauline's gaze. She nodded, understanding. I mouthed, "only half-way," and she grinned.

We, all three, climbed into the truck, me in the front and him and her in the back. He was telling me this and that when I heard a zip then a, "whoa," and I climbed out of the truck. About two minutes later she climbed out leaving him fumbling in the back seat.

He got out of the truck with a totally confused look on his face, and a hard on straining his jeans. I guessed Mike Love was about forty. The word about him was he went to Vegas three times a year and got broke on gambling and white hookers every trip. So much so that his son, who is my age, started going to Vegas with him. His son slowed up the gambling, but he couldn't do nothing about the white hookers who was

57

still tearing a hole in Mike Love's ass.

The son, whose mama is white, even though him and his daddy is black as asphalt, gave up on correcting the hooker behavior. The word is Mike Love goes to Vegas four times a year and tricks off fierce.

While trying to act like he didn't have a hard on, Mike Love asked, "So you like the truck?" The man was one of those people whose face shows they emotions. No matter what came out of that man's mouth, I could tell that getting some pussy was all that was on his mind. He was looking at Pauline real thirsty like. The look made me nervous for her. If it wasn't nobody but him and her in the garage, he would have raped her.

"Yeah, I do like the truck."

"It's brand new, like I said. Got it from D.C., so you ain't gonna have no local problems with it. Less than two thousand miles on it. Still smells new."

"I don't know about that. It smelled like pussy in there to me."

"Huh?"

"Smells like you been fucking in that truck."

"Naw, you crazy. It didn't smell like that."

He was showing every tooth in his head, and his hand had fallen to his crotch.

"Let me get it for eight grand, and it could."

"Huh?"

"Let me get the Lexus for eight, and Ms. Pauline will get back in the truck with you and spend as much time as you like."

He looked around the warehouse car wash at the squares in the front and said, "People will see."

"You can't see through the tinted windows, and them seats let

58

back."

"You want me to pay two grand for some pussy?"

"No. No way. I want you to sell me the truck for eight grand, and to show my appreciation for your consideration and love for E.O.G., I am going to let you do whatever you want to my freshest, never been on the strip ho'e, out of respect for the business we do."

"Never been on the strip?"

"Days of the week still on her Disney panties."

"I can fuck her in the ass?"

He was a nasty motherfucker.

"If that's what you want."

"Deal, but me and her got to go in the office. I ain't doing it in the truck."

That was cool with me, because I didn't want my truck smelling like asshole. I peeled him off eight grand, and he handed me the papers and the keys. He and Pauline went up to the office for about thirty minutes. She came down looking no worse for wear and smiling. How ho'es can take it up the ass I will never know.

She got back into the truck and handed me a fresh hundred-dollar bill. "The owner of the carwash wanted a date, too."

"That's a good ho'e. Give your daddy a kiss on the cheek."

When we pulled out of the carwash, darkness had come to the city, and it was only six ten by the Lexus clock. The days were winter time short. I decided to swing by the clubhouse and get Billie so she could go to my daddy's for dinner too. The ho'e would be crying for a month if I left her out.

Before I pulled onto the Avenue, I heard the E.O.G. call. I looked to the left and saw ten soldiers in format. I looked to the right and saw the same. They must have seen me go into the carwash. The ten to my left marched out and blocked north bound traffic. The ten to the right marched out and blocked south bound traffic. Hotel Johnny, a clique member under Founder Six, Tray Six's daddy, nods his head and offers me the avenue. I throw up the E through the driver's window and take the street in my new Lexus truck. Some days ain't shit sweeter than being E.O.G.

*

When we got to the spot, Tommy Locke was coming out of Billie's room fully dressed and sweating like a runaway slave. His eyes were bucked open, crack-head wide. When I got to him, crack smoke was all around him. I smelled it plain as day. I didn't wait for him to lie. I was trying to hit him in the gut, but since he was taller I caught him in the dick. He bent over, and I threw a left upper cut that caught his ass square in the chin, and that laid his ass out right in front of Billie's room. I was standing over him, stomping him in the stomach, when Tray Six walked in.

"What the fuck," he screamed, and pushed me away.

"This mother fucker been smoking crack!"

"What!" Tray Six dropped to him and started bombing him to the chest with heavy rapid blows. I don't know where Benny Moon came from, but suddenly he was next to me kicking Tommy all about his thighs, ribs and head.

All it took was one motherfucker smoking crack to fuck up the whole clique. We all knew it. We had all seen it, clique after clique fell to a smoker. A fucking crack-head was not to be trusted. Tommy Locke was saying fuck us, so we were saying fuck him.

"Look at his fucking thumb." Tray Six was holding his hand up.

60

The thumb was callused. That meant he'd been flicking lighters to crack pipes for a while.

"This motherfucker is a crack-head."

He threw such a blow that I know it broke Tommy Locke's jaw.

"Strip his ass down and tie him to the chair," came from Benny Moon.

In his pockets we found two crack pipes, a glass cylinder, a metal, antennae along with three Bic lighters, and two eight-balls; half of one gone and one was still sealed.

"Call his daddy! Call his motherfuckin' daddy before we do it," I said to stop Tray Six who had already pulled and cocked his pistol.

E.O.G. law; 'One to the head, because you already dead' for crack smokers.

I made the call. "Founder Locke, this is Dai Break Jones. We request your honorable presence in regards to your son . . . Sir? Yes, it is in regards to that . . . Yes, sir, we are aware of the law . . . Yes, sir, my father is at home . . . We will wait for your honorable arrival. "

I went to Tray Six and took the gun from his hand, "Nobody touches him until they arrive."

"Sounded like he knew." Benny Moon had sat on the couch. I looked for Pauline and saw her and Billie in the bedroom with the door open. Billie didn't look high at all. I thought about what she told me a couple of months ago about Tommy trying to pay her in crack rocks, and trying to get her to hit the pipe. I didn't want to look at her so I said, "You ho'es got to go. Don't come back until the motherfuckin' mornin', after ten, and don't fuckin' come back broke." They left without a word.

Duran came in first with his pistol drawn; behind him were my daddy and Founder Locke. We all stood when they entered the spot. That was my daddy's first time at our clubhouse. He was still in the black mink and the leather Rocka-Wear sweat suit he wore to the doctor. Founder Locke was in dark brown leather trench and brown gators. Whenever you saw a founder on the street they looked rich.

Founder Locke had a black pistol with a silver silencer in his hand, and his red, tired eyes were on Tommy Locke, his second to the oldest boy. Founder Locke had seventeen kids by three different women who all lived in the same house, out of his seventeen kids, fifteen of them were boys.

"Did anybody here see him smoking that shit?" was his question to us.

"No," all three of us answered.

"I just saw him high, and coming out of Billie's room surrounded by crack smoke."

"He had pipes and a open eight-ball of crack in his pocket," came from Tray Six.

"But nobody saw him smoking?" he asked again.

"No, sir," we three answered again.

Founder Locke looked at my father with a look I couldn't read. I didn't know if he was asking for a pass or agreeing to hold up the law. A thug was real glad Tray Six did not put one in his head because even founders found it hard to make the decision. The law was clear, 'One to the head because you already dead.' But none of us said a thing. Tommy Locke hadn't mumbled a sound since we tied him up and gagged his ass, but his eyes was open and on his daddy and mine.

Duran walked behind him and put his pistol to Tommy Locke's head and recited the law. "One to the head because you already dead."

It was going to be either Duran or Tommy Locke who would be put into the Divine Emperors position of the first clique of E.O.G. when my daddy stepped down. And I believe that thought was on everybody's mind. If Duran pulled the trigger it would be him.

But he dropped the gun to the floor and said, "I beg you, most honorable sirs, for his life. He is my second soldier, with Dai Break being my first. He is my left hand in all things. Without him I would be crippled. If you take him, you end our clique."

I didn't see it coming, but I heard the metallic zips. Founder Locke put three in his second oldest son's head and told Duran, "He was already gone. Promote a new second soldier. No clique depends on one. You know that!" He walked out of the spot, with my daddy following.

"Benny Moon," my daddy yelled back, "Come . . . take us home."

They left what remained of Tommy Locke for us to clean up. Seeing him there with his head opened up made me think about that rapist Manny. He was my first body. I shot his ass five times in the back of the head while he was raping Babee in the alley behind her daddy's house. One of the bullets went through him and ended up in her shoulder. She talks about that today, me shooting her, but not the rape.

We should have put some plastic under the chair. Blood, brains and little pieces of head was scattered all over the floor. Cleaning Tommy Locke up was going to take some work. His blood was already starting to stain the wood floor. I went to the cabinet under the sink, looking for cleaning stuff and garbage bags.

"Hold up on that," came from Duran. He pulled his phone from his pocket.

"Pete, its Duran. Need your clique to do a cleanup at Dai Breaks.

Be here in five minutes."

Peter was Tommy Locke's older brother. If any beef was to come from his death it would come from him. His clique was directly under ours in rank. They were older, but we generated more money, and Peter was the only one of royal blood in his clique. Our whole clique was all royalty. Some thought that was why we stayed at the top, because we got better work from our daddy. That was bullshit. We were the top earners because Duran, he kept us working.

We could order any clique beneath us to do whatever, but we seldom did. Duran calling Peter was a squash move, stopping trouble before it got started.

Tray Six walked over to me, "He killed his son for E.O.G. law. Founder Locke is hard all the way through."

"Yeah, he did it for the law, but I think he was stopping one of us from doing it too. If Duran had done it, thugs would have said he did it to move up."

Duran snapped, "Fuck what thugs woulda said! Founder Locke did it for the law. Ain't no telling who gonna be Divine Emperor. That time is a long way off. What he did was for E.O.G. We can't have crack-heads within the organization. Son, brother, nobody can smoke that shit. The founders know that. Every soldier knows that.

"It's money making poison. We sell it to fools that choose that death. To weak motherfuckers who are expendable to our wealth. Tommy knew that. We all know that. It is to be sold, not used. I hate the shit. Sometimes I wish we would have never got into it, but what is, is.

"Tomorrow, Dai Break . . . me, my daddy and your daddy are flying out to California to meet with some Columbians . . . They are

64

gonna take E.O.G. to the next level in this drug shit. We about to get the product raw, straight from the manufacturer, from Columbia to E.O.G hands. Cocaine, not crack. We finna be too big to have weak links. Founder Locke knows that. He did what he did for E.O.G."

He kicks the chair holding Tommy Locke's corpse. "This motherfucker was a weak link."

We three were standing in the kitchen looking at what was our friend, our boy since birth. We stood looking at his bloody face, his caved in forehead and missing eyeball. And none of us dropped one fucking tear.

It took Peter and his clique ten minutes to ring the clubhouse doorbell. Tray Six let the five of them in. Duran had us put up our pistols. He said it wasn't to be like we was challenging them or defending ourselves. What was done was done, and Peter was going to have to accept it.

They came with plastic drop cloths, mops, buckets, rags, plastic gloves, cleanser and a gallon of purple soap. Peter, who is tall as Duran, said, "My father called me. I know who it is." And he didn't say shit else.

Him and his clique went into the kitchen and got busy. When they finished, Tommy Locke and the chair he was tied up in was gone. The purple soap they used darkened the whole kitchen floor, but I saw no traces of blood. Daisy was probably going to trip on the darker floor, but fuck, the place was clean, and smelled like a truck stop bathroom.

And just like that, Tommy Locke was no more.

Chapter Seven

When I walked into my daddy's house, Daisy was sleep in his front room on the beige leather pit. His flat screen, which he had mounted on the wall, was on the History Channel. The program was about Hannibal, an African general who my daddy said marched elephants from Africa to Rome. He was sitting in the recliner part of the pit, in his robe and thick socks. On the table next to him was a saucer that held a little meat and some rye crackers.

He nodded his bald head toward Daisy and said, "Her and Cheryl cooked a roast, potatoes, and some squash. I left it on da stove for ya. Be sure to clean it up. Cheryl wasn't a bit happy about me leavin' dat food out."

Cheryl was the first girlfriend my daddy had living with us. Then her and my daddy broke up, and I never saw her again, until Daddy hired her last year as our live-in maid. He says there is nothing else to her living with us other than her being the maid. But I know there is more to the relationship, since more days than not, I wake up to her in his bed. And after she moved in, he stopped entertaining female company and going out with other women.

My daddy loves to go out stepping every Thursday night. He dresses to the nines: beaver hats, tailor-made suits, 'gators, the whole thing. He matches from head to toe. And each week he took a different woman out stepping, but that all changed after Cheryl moved in. Now it's only him and her on Thursday nights, and she dresses just as sharp as him. She looks like nobody's maid on Thursday nights.

I sat on the cushion next to him. "So, you going to Cali tomorrow?"

He patted me on my thigh. "Yeah, I wanted you to go with us. Dat's what I wanted to talk to you about, but we now bought da tickets. Thangs got kinda crazy with all dat Tommy mess, so I let it go. You'll be at da next meetin'." He nodded his bald head towards me. I noticed gray stubble on the sides of his head and face. He needed to shave his dome.

People say my daddy growls more than talks because his voice is scratchy, and he grumbles his words. He told me some punk hit him in throat with a bat when he was a kid, and his voice has been rough ever since. He wasn't asking me to be at the next meeting in California, he was telling me I would be there.

"How is founder Locke?"

He didn't answer me right away. He ran his hands across the stubble on his head and sighed.

"Dai Break, da man killed his son. He ain't happy."

Changing the subject, I pointed toward Daisy. "She been sleeping long?"

"Since I got home from yo' place. She a smart woman; talked to her at da store and while she was cookin'. She thinks different dan most ho'es, hell different dan most people. I like her. Cheryl likes her too, and you know dat don't happen much. Da two of dem was in da kitchen goin' on like old hens. Go eat. Da food is good."

He was through talking because the show was back on. I stood and walked into the kitchen. Daddy bought the house on Forty-eighth and Forrestville when I turned fifteen. He had it gutted and totally remodeled. He put up a nine foot cast iron fence, and keeps four posted soldiers around it, two in the front and two in the back, even when he is not home.

His kitchen is too fly. Cheryl had all chrome everything put in. Double stove, refrigerator, sinks, microwave, dishwasher. All of it had that dull shine. She put an island in the middle, so people could sit on tall stools and eat, but on the other side she has a table that could seat six. Her and daddy usually eat over there. I eat on the island.

The roast and potatoes was damn good. The squash was okay. I put a lot of black pepper on it. A pimp was washing the dishes by hand when I heard, "So, you made it back, huh?" It was Daisy wiping sleep out of eyes while standing in the kitchen doorway.

"Yep, here is where you see me, ain't it?"

"Yes, Daddy, here is where I see you."

"The food was good . . . and my daddy said you was smart . . . and he said Cheryl likes you."

She walked into the kitchen and stood at the island.

"I like her, too. She reminds of my mama."

Daisy had never said a thing to me about her mama.

"How?"

"The way she talks, things she says."

I cut the water off and put my plate in the dish rack.

"Where your mama at?"

"She's dead. My stepdaddy killed her when she caught him raping me. She tried to fight him but he was a man. He broke her neck and raped me again with her lying on the side of the bed, dead."

"Damn, that's fucked up."

I walked over to the island and gave the ho'e a hug, because she needed one, and pulled her over to the table and we sat down.

I was tired and sleepy as hell, but it was time to talk to my bottom.

"What happened to the sick fuck?" I asked while holding her hand.

"When my brother came home from work, he found mama dead and me naked and crying. He went into the bathroom where my step daddy was on knees praying to God. My brother tore the towel rack from the wall and beat him to death with it. He's doing life right now at Statesville. I left before the people from the state could put me in a home, and I been on the streets every since."

I know a lot of chicks with the same type of story. Punk ass men rape females all the fucking time, but to be raped with your dead mama lying next to you, now that was some fucked up shit. Daisy had had it hard, no doubt. I put my other hand on top of hers. I couldn't think of shit consoling to say, so I asked a question.

"So, you went straight from living with your mama, to the strip?"

"No, not really. I fell into ho'ing because I wasn't scared to do it. Men no longer worried me. I realized they could kill me, but so could a speeding car or cancer, everybody dies. The first man I stayed with was a bus driver. I caught his bus the night my mama died. I was in my gown and winter coat, and no bus fare. He was barely nineteen. His daddy had got him a job he didn't want because it was time for him to move out on his own.

"I stayed with him until his babies' mama came back from Memphis with they twin boys. He paid me fifty dollars every night I was there. He was surprised that every night he came home from work I was still there. I stayed because I was homeless.

"When I left him, the thought came to me that I was ho'ing. He fed me, fucked me and paid me. I walked up to Forty-seventh Street and started car hopping. That morning, Sweet Black pulled me in and I was with him until I got with you.

"I thought about going to my grandmama's in Detroit, but I don't

69

never do much more than think about it. I'll be nineteen in two weeks. I been ho'ing since I was fifteen. Seen a lot of sad shit, been to some fly places, and tricked with a couple of stars. I had a mink coat, and now I have a real diamond tennis bracelet. The life ain't been all bad, but right now, at this moment, I feel like a tired old ho'e, and I'm barely nineteen."

She was looking at me hard, like I was supposed to say something to her. I kissed the ho'e on the check and gave her the nod to keep talking.

"Tray Six got me to thinking when he came up to the hospital to bring me some clothes and the bracelet. I want to get my G.E.D., Daddy. I got good grades in school. And he said that with my mama dead I could get State aide and go to college after I got my G.E.D.

"There is another life out there, Daddy, a life that don't revolve around tricks and sucking dicks to eat. I called up to the library before I left the hospital. They got the G.E.D. class on Mondays, Wednesdays and Fridays, in the morning and at night. I got good grades in school, Daddy."

Daisy was trying to look eye to eye with me, like she was trying to get me to understand something more than that she had had it hard. But a thug was tired. I saw that she needed to talk some more, so I sat quiet and tried to listen.

"How much longer will it be before I get AIDS, or shot in the head? I ain't scared. I just want that other life. The one I had before my step daddy took it from me. I was in the Upward Bound Program, Daddy. The one that gets high school kids ready for college, I was a fourteen-year-old junior in high school. I got promoted twice in grammar school, Daddy, skipped third and fifth grade. My brother was smart, too. His job was sending him to school at night for computer programming. My mama was a R.N.

"I can be good at anything, Daddy, anything I put my mind to. But I'm afraid that if I keep ho'ing, all I will ever be is a good ho'e. And that ain't what my mama wanted. It's more to me than being a ho'e, Daddy."

Then it hit my slow ass. The ho'e was talking about leaving me. A pimp like me couldn't have that. I took my hands from her hand and knocked the bitch upside her forehead. I stood up and started choking the ho'e. I put my hand across her mouth so she couldn't scream out, and pulled the ho'e up out the chair, and kneed the bitch in her butt bone. I slammed her down to the floor and stomped her in the chest. Then I drug the ho'e out my daddy's backdoor and past his two rear guards.

They looked shocked but didn't say a word. I drug the ho'e down the steps to the dark garage, pulled my keys out of the sweat pants pocket and opened the truck of my Chevy and tossed the bitch on top of the spare. I shut the trunk on the ho'e and yelled, "Dumb bitch."

I walked back upstairs without saying shit to the guards, didn't even look at them. I went back into my daddy's house and dropped into a chair at the kitchen table. The situation was Tray Six's fault, telling my ho'e about school. He got her that ass whipping.

I went upstairs and took a good hot shower, used plenty of body wash to scrub off two days worth of funk. Tired, I crawled naked under the covers and the fresh sheets that Cheryl put on my bed, and went to sleep.

When I woke up that morning I took another shower. My cornrows was getting a little loose, but it wasn't a hurry to get them redone. I dried off and stepped into a fresh pair of Fruit of the Loom boxer briefs and walked over to the closet.

I picked out a pair of black Coogi jeans, with the lime green and red pockets, and a lime green Coogi jersey. Slid into my Coogi boots with the lime green C on the side. I sprayed down with some Axe and went over to the bed and flipped up the mattress.

There I found the .45 and the box of shells Duran brought from Indiana. Two months ago he came back from Gary with ten clean .45s. I loaded up the clip and put the pistol in the small of my back. I went over to the dresser and grabbed my iPod, phone, and hung my E.O.G. chain around my neck. I pulled my red fox from the closet and slid into it.

Daddy was gone and Cheryl was in the kitchen. Cheryl is a skinny tall yellow woman, who in her day I'm sure had the thugs going. But with that head rag on her head, and in a light blue duster, she looked the part of my daddy's maid.

"How you be, Cheryl?"

"Oh, hey, Dai Break." She was bent down wiping down the pine wood kitchen cabinets with some lemon smelling oil.

"Is that your pretty truck out front?" she asked, standing to face me.

"Yep, I got it yesterday. You like it?"

I walked past her to the frig, opened it and didn't see any apples or grapes, so I closed it back.

"Yes, I do, it looks like the other one you were driving, just bigger and nicer wheels."

"It's a later model. How long my daddy been gone?"

"They left early this morning. I did your laundry, but since you wasn't here I went on and put the clothes up. Check to make sure everything is where you want it."

I wanted to move the .45 from the small of my back because it was digging into my left butt check, but Cheryl doesn't like to see guns, so I waited until I got out to the garage. I walked past her to the back door.

"See you later."

She was putting the cap back on the oil.

"You be careful out there, and be sure to call your daddy, check to make sure he landed okay."

When I got out on the porch the same guards were on duty. One of them looked like he wanted to say something, so I paused. He said nothing, so I kept walking. Most soldiers respect me, some don't. Soldiers move up in rank through earning and deeds. I was born to a position that they could never reach.

They can move up, but they can never be bloodline royalty. Five from the first hand will always be at the top. They are told this at first step induction, but some are still jealous. I can see it in they eyes. Most soldiers are poor as hell, and they become part of E.O.G. for a leg up, and they get it. They get hooked up into a family with over two-thousand soldiers.

The smart move is to get under a working clique with a smart leader, with somebody who directs you to money. Duran keeps our soldiers working, either with weed, rocks, or strong arm. Ain't no broke soldiers under us.

The Founders' clique has over two hundred personal soldiers; being a soldier to the Founders' clique is the quickest way to get noticed and get your own clique. The guard who almost said something to me was

73

about to be granted a clique under my daddy. A five man clique with fifty soldiers, the same amount of soldiers our clique has. Daddy liked the guard. That was why he got so many soldiers.

In the garage, I didn't hear a sound from Daisy. I hoped I hadn't killed the ho'e. The garage was new. Daddy had the old red brick one torn down. This one had bright lights, and when I flipped the light switch it was more like being in a basement than a garage.

When I opened the trunk Daisy was wide awake and looking at me crazy. Her eyes were red and she had dried up yellow snot under her nose and lip. I waited for the ho'e to say something. She was smart enough not to.

Looking at the mess she was, I thought about her just getting out of the hospital. And for a brief second, I felt like I might have been too hard on her. Then I remembered the ho'e was talking about leaving me, and that just wasn't part of the game. Not for a pimp like myself.

I looked at her and said, "Ho'e, as long as you are with me, all your fucked up ass brain should be working on is making my money. Bitch, the motherfucking future ain't a problem for you. Today is your gotdamn problem. One day at a mother fuckin' time. Fuck the future. Getting my money for the day! That is all your ass need to be thinking about. Fuck a G.E.D. Fuck a college. Ho'e, get my money! I'ma take care of everything you need in this life, and, bitch, if I don't give it to you, you don't fucking need it. I'm your motherfucking provider. I am your God on Earth, ho'e, and don't ever forget that. Now get your nasty ass in there and shower, and meet me out in the truck in ten minutes."

I helped her out of the trunk. Daisy fumbled in place but wasn't moving in a direction. She stutter stepped where she was. The ho'e was confused and totally disorientated.

"Get to moving!"

Yelling that at least got her out of the garage.

The ho'e made it up two back steps and collapsed onto the sidewalk, and rolled into the snow puking up yellow shit. The guard my daddy likes helped me get her up, but she couldn't stand on her own. I called her name a couple of times, but she didn't hear me. She didn't hear shit I said. I shook the ho'e, but all that did was make her throw up more.

From the back door, Cheryl yelled, "Take her back to the hospital. She still sick!"

The guard put her into the Chevy. Cheryl comes down the stairs and gets into the car without asking. When we get to the hospital they come straight and get Daisy. I guess Cheryl called ahead. I had them page Dr. Silverman.

After he examined Daisy he came to Cheryl and me in the crowded emergency room waiting area. He told us Daisy had experienced some type of psychological trauma, and that along with the return of the pneumonia, would require her to stay in the hospital. He looked to me. I pulled out the two grand savings I got from buying the Lexus and gave it to him.

Cheryl asked was Daisy conscious and could we see her. He answered no to both questions and pocketed the money. Cheryl didn't say a word on the drive home, and I didn't say goodbye once we got there. She just climbed out and went up the back steps into the house. I parked the Chevy back in the new garage. I went up front and I got into my new truck.

Maybe she did know what happened to Daisy the night before,

maybe she didn't; either way it wasn't her fucking business, nothing the maid should have been concerned with. It was a nice sunny winter day and wasn't shit going to make it cloudy for me.

Once I got into the truck I put the .45 under my seat and pulled my bankroll from my pocket. A thug needed to separate E.O.G. dope money from my cash. With Tommy Locke dipping like he obviously was, Duran was going to take a count, and I wanted my account to be on point. I'd sold two and a half eight-balls and a pound and a half of weed. I took two hundred of my money and added it to the dope money because of the half an eight-ball that the cop took from under my seat and kept. I had also been fronting Julia here and there and wasn't keeping track, the two hundred should cover everything. With the dope money out of my roll, I had fifty four hundred dollars. I wanted my ten grand back in the bank by Monday. That meant the goal was forty six hundred more. It was earning time.

I got that from my daddy, giving myself daily goals. Short-term goals, he calls them. Sometime they take a day, and sometime they take a week. If I make them happen in a day, a thug gets real happy, it's time to celebrate then. In the middle of my bankroll was the eye doctor's card, the trick that gave Billie a thousand dollars. If he had a thousand to give her, he should certainly have forty-six-hundred in the safe.

I could have pulled the job by myself, but I was a finger on the hand and it was more than me that ate from the palm, E.O.G. thinking. Duran wasn't due back until that Saturday night. And once he got back, we had to promote a soldier to the clique to be five. Benny Moon's brother, Heart, was next in line.

He had been Marshall to fifty soldiers for three years. It was his time. The word was he was going to get to pick five from the soldiers

76

rank and start his own clique, but shit changed with Tommy Locke's death, and he became part of us.

Chapter Eight

When I pulled up to the clubhouse, both Billie and my new white girl was getting helped out the back of a Benz limo. A long black limo driven by a tall black man, surrounded by a snow covered street in the middle of the 'hood, was a striking sight to see. The dude helping them had on a chauffer's uniform with cap and all. I stayed in the truck and watched as he gave Pauline a pat on her narrow booty, and Daisy a kiss on the check.

The driver was tall enough to be playing for the Bulls. The bib of his little black cap was reflecting the sunlight like a mirror. It made me remember how when we was kids we use to bounce the sun off broken pieces of mirror into the face of passing drivers. That was fun, especially if the driver slammed on the brakes and swerved.

The shiny capped driver got behind the wheel of the limo and pulled off, as he waved goodbye to my girls. I looked down at my big faced, diamond studded Cartier watch and saw it was eleven thirty. They had been out all night. My thought was, those ho'es had better have my money.

It turned out the limo driver was working an architects' convention at the McCormick Place Hilton, and thanks to him my ho'es had got the inside track on a good night's work.

"Three-hundred a pop, Daddy." Billie's tired eyes had a little twinkle in them when she reported on the rate.

"I turned five, and one of them only wanted to see me naked and a hand job. Ty, the limo driver really hooked us up. He had a suite, Daddy, a penthouse suite with a beautiful lake view. We had Champagne and grapes, and a tray of little finger sandwiches. The T.V.

78

was a big flat screen, and we ordered movies. I didn't get to watch none all the way through, but we ordered them. And Daddy you should have seen how many pillows they put on a bed. It was ridicules.

"Anyway, when we was between dates we was in that suite. It was nice. Ty is gay, and was working just as hard as we was. He got pissed off because he couldn't see the end of any of the movies. I mean he was really upset."

She slid out off her heels and held them in her hand. Billie was rattling off like she was geeked up on crack or something. She seldom talked that much. Whenever one of my girls did something out of the ordinary my antennas went up.

"That tall ass dude is a sissy?"

"Yep, and he was working harder than us," Pauline giggled. She was sitting on the end of the couch next to Billie. "He was taking Viagra pills and drinking ginseng bottles like crazy. I turned six dates, and he did more than me. He didn't sit down for thirty minutes the whole night."

Something was up with them. They wasn't high, but they both was nervous. Then it came to me that they was probably holding out on some cash

"Who handed y'all the money?"

Billie answered with, "That was the sweet part, Daddy. The bellhop would come up with the cash and a room key, which he gave to Ty. Then Ty would hand us the key and three hundred dollars, regardless of what we had to do in the room."

I was starting to see the problem.

"So the bell hop gave the cash to Ty, the limo driver, and he peeled you off three-hundred? Did you see how much the bellhop gave him?"

I knew the answer to question before I asked it.

Billie wasn't a girl who watched the money. She was more into the deed, the sex. And this was something I had gotten on her about before, 'watch the money,' I had told her time and time again.

"Not really, Daddy. Once he counted out the three hundred dollars I went to the trick's room," Pauline answered.

Billie's didn't say a word. Her eyes was on the coffee table.

That's why Daisy was my bottom. She would have known what Ty was getting in his hand.

"That sissy was pimping y'all, and getting my money!"

When I said that they both tensed up, I started to snap off right then, but I needed more information. The sissy got the best of them. My girls were just happy to get cut in on the three-hundred-dollar dates.

"And, Daddy, our room wasn't the only room the bell hop was going into. That little Chinese boy was going in and out of at least five rooms." Pauline was letting me know that at least she was paying attention.

"Really?" I said, trying to hide my anger. A pimp needed them to keep talking, and if they were relaxed they would remember more, and I needed all the information I could get, because the only hands that should have touched money my ho'es made, was mine.

"No joke, Daddy. He was on it, hopping in and out of them five rooms like he was delivering free shrimp fried rice."

Billie handed me a stack of twenties once we got inside the clubhouse. Sitting next to her on the couch, I began counting the money. It was thirty-two hundred dollars.

"How long is the convention in town?"

Another lick like that, and a pimp would get the ten grand back before Monday.

"Tonight is the last night, but Ty was saying it won't be as good as last night, because a lot of the architects fly out early in the morning and don't trick off before the flights. He's going back this afternoon around four."

Billie looked up at me. I smiled.

"He said he's going back in drag though," Pauline giggled again.

"Did one of y'all get the Chinese boy's number?" The question was to Billie.

"Nope, he wouldn't talk to us. He only talked to Ty."

I let her see the smile fall from my face. She was way too lax last night, and this Ty dude had played her good.

"You got Ty's number?"

"Nope, He said he would be back over here around four to get a lift back. We told him you would probably want us to go back. He doesn't work with the limo company tonight, so he won't have a car. The place he works for is right down the street, said he lives on the same block as the limo place." Billie leaned back against the couch and rested her head on the white wall. She let her eyes close.

"What was you thinking, Billie? How come you wasn't watching the money?"

She opened her eyes to me. She was dog tired and it showed.

"Daddy, I was so happy to get the three-hundred a trick that I didn't think past it."

I have told her countless times to watch the damn money. The situation was beyond me talking, something needed to be done to make my orders stick in her head. The limo driver Ty had gotten my money, and it was partly her fault.

Pauline, who seemed clueless to the seriousness of the way things were, said, "He told us the only time he ain't in drag is when he got to work for the limo service."

She stood up from the corduroy couch and stretched up towards the ceiling. Then she bent in half and touched her toes twice, and sat back on the couch and began to beat out a little rhythm with her palms on her thin thighs.

I took my eyes off of Billie. , "So he be ho'ing when he ain't driving the limo?"

"That's what he said, Daddy. Said he works Broadway, Madison, and Evanston," Pauline chirped.

"Y'all ever seen him before?"

Billie's gaze was at the front window. "Wouldn't know until I seen him in drag. Said he always be in a long blond wig."

I had to do something besides beating Billie. Obviously, beating her wasn't making my words stick. Ain't no telling how much loot they missed, because her ass wasn't watching the money. They might of got four-hundred a trick.

"Hundreds of ho'es be in long blond wigs. So he is a renegade?" Both of them got stiff again when I asked that.

Billie quietly answered, "I didn't think to ask him who he was with, Daddy, sorry." Again her eyes went down.

Yep, that motherfucker was a renegade. No way Billie didn't ask a ho'e who her pimp was, sissy or not. I had Daisy talking about getting out of the game, and the other two had spent the night working with a renegade. None of that was good news.

Renegades get ho'es to thinking they can be on they own, that they don't need a pimp. Ho'es see them tramps with money in they pockets, and then they start thinking they should have money in they pockets too. Renegades make ho'es question they happiness.

I needed to make a big move, one that would remind them of the benefits of being with Dai Break Jones. One that would remind them of how safe and happy they was with me. And I had to do something to shake Billie's non-listening ass up.

"You say this Ty dude stays down the street."

"Yes Daddy," Billie turned her head from the window to me.

"Come on," I ordered.

I had seen limos parked in a lot a couple blocks over. A pimp knew where to go, and it wasn't hard to spot the dude. He was still in his uniform and walking down the block. I pulled past him and parked at the end of the block and got out. I left the girls in the truck.

Wasn't nobody on the block but him and me, a bad situation for him. He stopped next to a raggedy blue and gray paneled van that had two flats on the street side. It must have been parked there for awhile because potato chip bags, some newspaper, brown paper bags and other windblown debris had gathered around the flat tires.

He was about ten steps away from me. He looked up and down the block before he walked to the back of the van and opened the door. The mark glanced right by me as I walked past him. He looked over me like I wasn't important, a stupid mistake. Once I passed him I drew my pistol and bum rushed back to him. A pimp attacked him from the rear. I hit his tall ass at the bottom of his skull with the butt of the .45. He immediately fell to his knees.

"Motherfucker, you can't take from me!"

His hands went to cover the spot I hit.

83

"Please, what is this all about? Please don't hurt me. I have nothing."

My daddy told me a begging man shouldn't have life. I have seen him slap panhandlers in the face. 'Weak motherfucker!' he'd yell and run them off with his pistol.

With the limo driver on his knees before me whimpering and begging, rage suddenly ran through me. I thought about Daisy trying to leave me. I thought about Tommy Locke turning crack head. I thought about them damn detectives taking my truck, and that cop taking my pistol. I thought about my ho'es giving him my money.

And the next thing I knew, a pimp had pulled the tiger, twice. I felt the .45 kick back solidly against the back of my palm. The shiny little cap was blown off his head.

Instinctively, I looked to my right and left. I looked up the block and down the block and saw no movement. His cap was the only thing in the street moving. It rolled next to his thigh.

With him slumped over I went through his pockets before the blood ran down from his head. Inside his jacket pocket was a cash fat envelope. I left him with two red spongy holes in the back of his head. I purposely didn't look at his face. It was more than likely ripped to shreds by the bullets' exits. The .45 was too hot to put back in the small of my back, so I picked up his shiny cap and covered the pistol with that as I jogged down the block to my truck.

When I got back to the truck both of them ho'es' eyes was wide open with fear. They heard the shots. They pimp had just blown a dudes head wide open in broad daylight. Yep, the renegade problem was solved. They knew who the man was.

To Billie, I said, "Bitch, the next time you don't watch the money

I'm gonna open up your skull just like that. Play with me if you want to."

When we got back to the clubhouse, I told both of them to go to bed and get some rest, 'cause we was going back to McCormick Place at four o'clock. They didn't hesitate to get out of my presence.

I sat on the couch and counted out the limo driver's money. He must have been screwing his ass off because that sissy had over seven grand. He had to have stolen from me. That seven Gs put me past the ten grand. A thug earned without breaking a sweat. I loved the pimp game.

Chapter Nine

My bankroll was so big I couldn't fold it; matter of fact, it wouldn't even fit into the limo driver's envelope. I got up and went into the kitchen. I looked in the cabinet under the sink and saw a box of zip-lock bags. I dumped my cash in one, and slid it down my briefs and behind my belt buckle.

I pulled out my cell phone and searched through the address book for Italian Fiesta's number. While ordering the pizza, Tray Six and Benny walked through the door, so I upped the order to four pizzas for delivery. I flipped the phone closed and told Tray Six, "I shouldn't have ordered your interfering ass shit."

Tray Six and Benny Moon stepped past me to get to the T.V. and the Xbox controllers. Benny Moon had a six pack of Miller Draft under each arm. He put both of them on the coffee table. Tray six sat in the chair and Benny Moon sat on the end of the couch. I noticed Tray Six had freshly done cornrows. His made me pat my own loosening ones. I stood up and walked around the table, thinking about opening the blinds.

"Wha-wha-wha-what is you talking about, Dai Break, damn? It's always som-som-som-something with you," he asked in response to me telling him he was interfering.

Tommy Locke was his boy, his best bud without a doubt. He spent more time with him than any of the rest of us. That was probably why he was at the clubhouse, instead of school or the library working on his book. Friday was a school day for him. He had afternoon classes, so there was no reason for him to be at the clubhouse, except for tripping over Tommy. The same with Benny Moon and the beer, he hardly drank. Part of me wanted to let the Daisy situation go until later, but the pimp in me wanted to get him straight as soon as possible, to make sure it didn't happen again.

"I'm talking about you putting school all up in Daisy's head. That's what I'm talking about."

He scooted to the edge of the chair with a controller in hand. Benny Moon sat up on the couch and grabbed the remote and a beer from the table.

"You n, n-n-n-need to go head on with that."

He dismissed me with a wave of his hand and put his attention on the blank television screen.

My mind went to Daisy, laid out in the snow puking her guts out because I had beat her due to what this babbling bastard told her.

"Nigga, you fuckin' with my money!"

The words came out harder and angrier than a pimp intended. I wasn't expecting to get mad. My plan was just to correct him. But when I thought about the whipping I gave Daisy because of what he planted in her head, the anger just came.

Tray Six looked up at me, then looked away, then back up at me. "If you f-f-f-feelin' how you soundin', bring it."

That wouldn't have been the first time me and Tray Six fought, but it would be the first time Duran wouldn't have been there to end it.

"She's good people, Dai Break. She be-be-be-better than ho'ing, ev-ev-ev-everybody see that but you. I like her, so yeah, I told her about sch-sch-sch-school. It's helping me. I figured it could help her, too. She got a brain and a kind heart. She should n-n-n-ot have to be selling her pu-pu-pu-pussy to make money. Everybody thinks that but you."

87

He was looking me in the eye while he was talking. When he finished talking, his eyes quickly went to the television which was still blank. I wanted to knock him upside his dome with the .45, because he was again dismissing me by turning his head. He figured since he was finished talking, the conversation was over.

Hitting him with the .45 would have been a bit much, but kicking him in the back of the head seemed okay. With them still sitting on the couch I was standing above both of them. I took a deep breath through my nose, took the air in slow, so it wouldn't be heard, and blew it out just as quiet. Duran taught us all to take deep breaths and think when we was mad. Doing this before saying something has helped me hundreds of times. I took a silent breath because my anger was my business. I have learned that people can play you when they know you are mad.

What I told him was, "Hell, all my girls is good people, Tray Six. Ain't shit wrong with ho'ing. They be getting my money, and ain't shit wrong with nobody getting my motherfucking money. But it is something wrong with motherfuckers interfering with my money getting got. So, stay outta my business, and stay the fuck outta my ho'e's ear."

Both of them longed haired thugs looked up at me like I was speaking French or something. As if what I was saying was ignorant as hell, just because she had cooked them a couple of meals. Those fools had gone soft, and they expected me to go soft, too. That wasn't happening. A thug was counting too much cash to go soft. Pimping was paying and I didn't need nobody butting in on my cash flow.

"You du-du-du-done?"

I would have mimicked his stutter, but he would have probably

88

shot me in the knee or something.

"Yeah, I'm done, motherfucker."

Benny Moon clicked on the T.V. and pulled a game from the inside pocket of his jacket. It was a boxing game.

"Oh yeah, five-o hotter than a motherfucker outside. Some fool got capped a couple blocks down." He put the game into the Xbox.

"Yeah, I know. I put that work in. The fool had seven grand for me. It's 'cause of him y'all getting pizza."

I grinned over to them, but I didn't get a smile back.

"E.O.G. work?" Benny Moon took off his orange and blue Bears leather jacket and started fumbling with one of the Xbox controllers.

"Naw, pimp game shit, damn it!" Suddenly, it came to me that I was going to have to get rid of the .45, and the pistol was brand new. When I glanced over to them they was both looking at me funny.

"What?"

"You standing there telling us you just earned s-s-s-seven grand and ain't nothing coming our way but some fu-fu-fu-fuckin' pizza?" Tray Six asked the question, but both of them was waiting for the answer.

I hadn't put my phone up, and the thought came to cancel the pizza order. The motherfuckers was being ungrateful and they was really getting on my damn nerves. I had enough going on without them adding shit to my day.

"I just told you it was pimp game related."

I kept my phone out and decided to call Heart to get rid of the .45.

Benny Moon put the controller on the coffee table.

"You know, I'm tired of hearing that shit! If it wasn't for us stomping that pimp ass nigga to death, yo' ass wouldn't be in the pimp game. So all this, 'it's pimp game related,' is bullshit. You think Duran

89

gonna come back from meeting with the Columbians saying, 'these my mama's people, so I ain't got to share this with y'all,'? Do you, Dai Break? You got to see how much you been tripping."

That was one of the few times both his eyes was in one direction, his crooked one, and his good one was in my face. He was waiting for me to answer.

Me and Benny Moon ain't never had hard words, never. Jealousy is not part of his nature. So hearing those words from him shook me a bit, made me listen for the truth in what he was saying. Yeah, I had come up from the pimping, and no, I hadn't thought about sharing the profits with the clique. The pimping work was all mine.

"When my daddy gave me half a tr-tr-tr-truck of big screens, I stuck one up in here and we all sold the rest and shared the money, like a clique is suppose to. Yo' ass being real motherfucking selfish with this p-p-p-pimping shit and we all been t-t-t-talking about it. Been waiting for yo' stingy ass to share the wealth."

If Benny Moon hadn't spoke first I would have totally ignored whatever complaints Tray Six had, because I was still mad about him getting in Daisy's ear. It was me that went out that afternoon and got the seven grand. I put the slugs in the limo driver's head. I was the one that had been working with my girls 24/7; me, myself, and I.

"You motherfuckers ain't sharing in the work," I spit out at them.

Me, and only me, was running the streets at wee hours of the motherfucking morning. Me, and only me, was motivating them ho'es to get out and get my money 24/7. Me, and only me, worked my way inside them ho'e's heads so they thought of me as God. Tray Six stood a better chance at making a tomcat fetch than he did at getting a quarter of my pimp money.

"You ain't never asked nobody to share in the work. But I tell you this, you blew a motherfucker's head open today, right? If the police come up in here, we all going to jail! Did you think about the weed and crack we got stashed in this place? No, you didn't. You just went out and did what you wanted to do, like always. And that shit is getting old. You making our spot hot for your own selfish profit."

Benny Moon must had forgot that the clubhouse came through me. With Duran gone, I knew the situation wasn't going to get settled. My thought was to drop sixty bucks on the table for the pizza and leave, come back around four, pick up the girls, and ignore the whole situation.

"Yo' ass the only one r-r-r-riding around in a new truck with seven grand cash in your pocket! We the number one clique in E.O.G., but you the only one looking like n-n-n-number one!"

Don't hate the player, hate the game is what I wanted to say.

"So, it's about the truck! You pissed about the fucking new truck?"

"No! I am pissed about yo' stingy ass. One hand, nigga, five fingers to a hand, five equal fingers. Yo' pimping got you b-b-b-bigger than any other finger on the hand. Cain't no-no-no-nobody else go out and buy a new motherfucking truck the same day the po-pos take one from 'em. Nobody but yo' ass, and th-th-th-that shit ain't right." He tossed his controller on the table with Benny Moon's.

Then it started to make sense as to why Tray Six had been telling Daisy about school. He was trying to sabotage my cash flow. Jealousy was running all through the man's brain. I was earning too much, shining too bright. My extra earnings, along with Tommy Locke's death had pushed him to the point of snapping. And the same thing was probably true with Benny Moon. We had lost one of five, and our

91

leader was out of town. We was all tripping.

I did two things. First, I thought about what Duran would do. Then I asked myself would I expect one of them to kick in if they had been earning independently. But when I looked at both of them, I realized that they would never have a real hustle outside the clique, not that they couldn't, but it was a loyalty thing with them. They liked earning together, and before pimping, I did, too. Nobody in the clique had ever done anything independent but me.

They had a point, and thinking about it wasn't helping the seven grand stay in my pants. I pulled up the zip-lock bag from behind my belt buckle, pulled the seven grand from it and split it into five piles, fourteen hundred apiece. I picked my pile and turned my back on the table. It was the right thing to do. We was going to have to meet with Duran about my everyday pimping money, though.

"Why five piles?" Benny Moon asked.

"A blessing for whoever gets promoted up."

I put the Ziploc bag back behind the belt buckle. "You motherfuckers paying for the pizza."

My girls are going to have to be clever ho'es to make up that seven grand. A goal is a goal.

I flipped the phone open again and dialed Heart's number. "What's up, dude? Send a solider to our clubhouse to make a lake drop for me . . . Naw, not you. It's too hot over here. I said send a soldier. Peace out."

When I turned back around, two of the four piles was gone, and they had started the game. The situation was over, at least for the time being.

I flipped the phone closed and asked Benny Moon, "Did you tell

Heart he was coming up?"

He was cracking his knuckles and popping his neck like he was getting ready for a real fight, instead of a video game.

"Nope, I'ma wait till it's certain."

"Who else would it be?" I walked over to the front window and opened the blinds for a few reasons: one, to see the pizza man when he pulled up; to keep a eye out of for five-o; and, to see the solider when he got there.

"Shit, I don't know. It could be him, but it might be Midnight."

"Midnight just got to be a marshal." I counted three police cars rolling by in the short time that I was at the window.

"Yeah, but he is earning big time."

"How?" I turned around from the window to face them because I always want to hear about people earning. I have never been scared of new opportunities.

"Little thug got a Ecstasy connect. Don't he, Tray?"

"Ye-ye-ye-yeap. Some dude he went to highschool with turned him on. My lil' brother making mad paper. They might give him a clique for di-di-di-distribution 'stead of moving him over to us. E-e-e-especially since Duran and his daddy working things out with his mama's people. We gonna be all over that m-m-m-move. We can't do that and the ecstasy. I think they g-g-g-gonna give Midnight a crew and put Heart with us."

What he was saying made sense, but I didn't offer a comment either way. I walked back over to the couch.

"You think that thing with the Columbians going to be that big?"

"Oh, hell yeah." Benny Moon moved the game ahead. He picked Muhammad Ali and Tray Six picked Mike Tyson.

I didn't sit on the couch. Instead, I went back into the kitchen and got a green plastic garbage bag, and wrapped the .45 up in it. Then I went through the numbers on my phone and looked to see if I had missed a call from my daddy. I hadn't, so I called him. The phone rang seven times and he didn't answer, so I hung up.

When I got back to the front room I found myself looking around for Tommy Locke. I damn near asked where he was, but then I remembered. His ass was dead.

Chapter Ten

I was looking for a hoopty, but the solider rolled up in a maroon Ford F150. I walked out to him instead of having him come into the house. He opened the passenger door, but I didn't get in. I placed the wrapped pistol on the front seat and told him, "Be careful."

By the time I made it to my truck he had already made it off the block. The sun was still giving us a pretty decent afternoon. I was pulling my truck keys from my pocket when the blue and white squad car rolled up on me. It was only one cop in the car. A skinny, doodoo brown officer who winked and blew me a kiss. It was the same motherfucker who took my .9mm and the crack from under my truck seat. What did he want?

The window rolled down and he said, "Get in, Dai Break Jones."

The pimp that I am, was not about to be seen in the front seat of a squad car. Without bending down to the window I said, "Not comfortable doing that officer."

His radio announced a fire on Forty-third and Cottage. He turned the volume down. "Meet me in five minutes at the Dunkin' Donuts on King Drive." The words jumped out the window at me as he pulled away from me and my truck.

I have never liked anybody telling me what to do. Following orders always gave me cause to pause, and those orders came from a cop, so a pimp was a little confused on what to do next. I paced alongside my truck a couple of times asking myself questions. Why did he wink at me both times? Had he turned in my pistol and dope? Was he trying to shake a pimp down? Should I go back into the clubhouse and get somebody to go with me?

"Fuck it."

I climbed into the Lexus and pulled down the visor against the sun, and drove to Dunkin' Donuts.

*

Outside the doughnut shop was the doodoo brown cop's squad car and a black GMC Denali. When I walked past the Denali I saw two white men behind the tinted windows, in sunglasses and suits. The sun was bright, but it wasn't shining inside that truck. It didn't cause them to wear sunglasses. An ice cold wind whipped across the parking lot.

I stopped at the door to the store. The situation didn't feel right, but I proceeded in making the bell at the top of the door jingle.

Inside the doughnut shop was a hazel eyed blond sales clerk and the cop. I had never seen the clerk before. A pimp gave her a little smile, because I liked the stern, serious look on her face, but she didn't return my smile at all. She stood behind the cash register looking as mean and unapproachable as a police dog. Her look added to my bad feeling.

The doodoo brown cop was sitting at the third table from the door, facing the window. The motherfucker was smiling at me, like we was family and it was Thanksgiving Day. I stopped after three steps in, and really considered turning around and leaving.

"Come, Dai Break." He half-way stood from his chair. "Have a seat." With a wave of his hand he offered me the chair directly across from him.

I used to like that doughnut shop. It was one of my favorite places to go to in the early afternoon; loved the candy smell of the place. It reminded me of the neighborhood candy-house that was across the alley from where I grew up. Mrs. Kelly sold candy, chips, cookies, pops, and she baked cupcakes. She sold the cupcakes two for a quarter and they was good, always soft, way better than Donuts'.

I went to Dunkin' Donuts almost every other day. I liked to just chill with a couple of toasted coconut ones and a large coffee, but a pimp doubted that I would ever be coming back to the place. The cop ruined it for me.

I sat across from him at the table by the window and asked, "What's with you dude?"

Still smiling, he pulled out a cell phone and handed it to me. On the small screen I saw myself. Me, with the limo driver on his knees in front of me, then I saw his shining cap blow off. The scene looped and played again.

I didn't know what to do except to keep watching the loop. My heart started beating loud in my ears. It was all I could hear. My first thought was to pull my pistol and take the phone. But I remembered I didn't have a pistol. The next thought was to run, but my legs wouldn't budge.

With a bass drum beating in my head, and stone legs, my mouth said, "That ain't me."

I barely heard the laughter through the beating, but it got louder as the drum lessened. The cop was laughing in my face. His mouth was open so wide that I saw two silver fillings inside his head. He had one on the left at the front, and the other was on the right way in the back. He suddenly stopped laughing, and wasn't even smiling.

"Well, you find me another five foot eight lesbo pimp, wearing the same colorful clothes and fox jacket that you're wearing and I'll talk to her, but until then . . . I got you. You are mine until I decide to let you go, or I should say ours."

97

As if on cue, the bell on the door jingled, and in walked the two white guys from the Denali. One of them I knew as Brent, one of Julia's friends that I sold crack to. I needed to be gone for real. I stood, but the doodoo brown cop said, "Sit down."

And I did. I put his phone on the table with the loop still going.

The two suits sat at the table with us. Brent nodded his head toward me with half a smile. A fucking undercover narc. I wondered if Julia knew. My eyes went to the clerk who came from behind the cash register with a blue tool box in her hand. She went over to the door, locked it and flipped the Open/Closed sign to Closed, and joined us at the table.

A pimp was fucked, and I knew it.

The doodoo brown cop looked at me. He had a sloped forehead. If a penny was rolled from the top of his head down his forehead it would take flight across the room. He had to have been teased hard when he was a kid. I looked at the phone on the table. The loop was still playing. The lime green pockets on my jeans did stand out.

Doodoo Brown scooted his chair closer to the table, "I thought we had you good enough with the northside sales, but then I pulled the crack and pistol from your truck, but then you helped us out even more when you went and killed Tyrone Jefferies in broad daylight. It was like you were applying for a DEA snitch position. I couldn't have asked for better grip on a C.I. A murder case. Dai Break Jones, you are going to be working for us until there is peace in the Middle East."

I saw him waiting for me to say something, but wasn't nothing to say. A pimp tried to nudge the table. If it would have moved, I would have used it to break out the window and run, but it was bolted to the floor.

But then what? It was Duran's words inside my head; sit still and listen.

The white man that was closest to me, Brent, asked, "You had no idea we were following you, huh? I thought you made us this morning when you left the hospital, but I guess not. Not if you are committing murder on film. What, we got three different angles on the shot?" He looked like a narc to me. I don't know why I didn't see it before.

"Two," the other white man in a suit put in. "Rich didn't get the kill shot, but he got her running up on the victim." He was grinning and shaking his head. "I couldn't believe you did that. But later I realized that if we hadn't had you under surveillance you might have gotten away with it. Maybe it wasn't so extreme after all."

He was what my daddy called a fair-haired boy, blond with blue eyes, but his hair was thinning. An all-American poster boy, except for his bald spot and broken nose.

"Where did you get the heart to pull the trigger in broad daylight? What were you thinking?"

That question came from the sales clerk who had brought the plastic blue tool box to the table with her.

"That's it. She wasn't thinking. Couldn't have been," said Doodoo Brown. "I think it is the whole E.O.G. gangster mentality that has her mind twisted. They all think they are above the law, until the law touches them." He sent me a wink across the table.

That wink brought a very clear thought to my head. Yes, they had me cold, but they didn't have my .45. It was in the lake. Maybe I wasn't so fucked. They didn't have a weapon. That thought, however, was only good for half a second.

Brent placed the garbage bag-wrapped forty-five on the table, as if he was reading my mind. I damn near lost my breath. The bass drum went off again and the table got real crowded.

Looking at the sales clerk, but talking about me, Brent said, "Chicago P.D. sure wants her bad. That detective Dixon is looking to pin whatever he can on her. He wants her off the streets. He thinks she has an influence on the community, and locking her down will shake up a few Dai Break Jones wannabes. He might get to be a problem."

Throat clearing was heard from Doodoo Brown. "It could be time to bring him into the operation. He and his partner appear to be honest. We will see."

Dixon was the homicide dick I met at headquarters, after the uniformed police yanked me out of my truck. Yeah, he did want a pimp bad.

"So, where are we working her first?" the fair-haired boy asked.

"Right here as planned, using her on that Columbian connection. Intel has her father already in possession of thirty keys. By the time he gets the load here, Chicago P.D. should be informed and well tempted. At that point we work her in."

He talked like it was a certainty that I was going to go along with whatever. His certainty kind of had me shook, made me feel like wasn't nothing a pimp could do about whatever they had planned. He was talking like he told the Chicago Police what to do, and it became real clear to me that they was into us, the E.O.G., deep. They knew my business, and my daddy's business.

"How do we connect her?"

"We don't. That's the confidential informant's job, not ours. A good C.I. makes the connect. She's going to have to make a big splash with those kilos. Then he will approach her. And based on his past history, she won't have to wait long." He pulls a folder from the brief case on the floor.

"Lieutenant Forrest will more than likely come at her after she moves the first kilo, and with what we already have on him, it will only take one transaction."

His breath smelled like Listerine-- the original, not the fruity ones-- but they were all paying attention to him despite his medicine breath. It seemed like he was the boss. Doodoo Brown cop was running things.

"You're right. Once she moves a kilo, he will be all over her with the modified product, forcing her to sell the confiscated coke," the fair head boy said to the table while stretching his arms. When he finished stretching, we all watched him loosen his baby blue neck tie. "And that's the lock right there. Once we got him passing that cocaine, we got him."

"Yep, we can put him out to pasture with the forced distribution. And that will be that. Another crooked cop sent up state." Doodoo Brown said that directly to me, like I was part of they team. He picked up the phone with the loop playing and put it inside his pants pocket without cutting it off.

"You must be really tired of this detail. How long you been under here, eight, nine months?" the sales clerk asked him.

"Ten . . . and I am more than ready to peel off this uniform and dump that squad car and kiss this dingy city goodbye. If little Ms. Dai Break Jones does what's expected, I'll be back in D.C. in less than sixty days. Chicago and Forrest is the last of the altered cocaine. It was a good assignment. Four major cities and, so far, nine high ranking police officials in prison. It wasn't a bad six years."

"Are you going to stay in field operations?" She asked.

"That's a joke right? Nope, I'm leaving all this," he spreads his arms over his head, "to ambitious youngsters like yourselves."

"Should we move her after the trial?" Brent asked him.

"That will be your call, but I don't see why. Forrest will be tried in Virginia, like the others. We are not involving Illinois in this at all. And besides, one does not know who he will turn on to lessen his sentence."

"You still hoping it will go higher than Forrest?"

"Yes."

"Give me your phone," the cashier said to me.

"Why?"

They had been talking about me as if I wasn't there. Talking all over me like I wasn't shit, and it was getting to me.

"Because I told you to." She put that police dog look on a pimp as if it meant something to me.

I was about to show her how little the look meant by grabbing her by the throat. All the shit was piling up on me, and I needed some space in my head. Fighting has always aired out my head.

"Give her the phone," came from Doodoo Brown. My attention went to him. At that point, I really didn't give a fuck whose neck I took hold of, so I jumped for him. The chrome .357 came up so smooth that I had to smile even with it at my forehead, "Sit your big ass down and give her the phone."

I sat and pulled the phone from my pocket and spun it on the table. She reached into the tool box and pulled out some tools and opened my phone. "What I am doing is converting this phone to a D.E.A. device that will allow us to track you and contact you at all

102

times. The phone will record twenty-four hours a day regardless of if you turn it on or not. It does not have to be on for us to contact you through it. It will work like a two way. Taking out the battery will not disconnect the device. No one will be able to detect the recording equipment, so don't worry about people looking for a bug. You will not have to take the phone out of your pocket for it to record. Basically, all you do is what you have always done with your phone. You no longer have to charge it for your normal phone functions or pay the bill. The number and all other features stay the same."

She put it back together and slid it to me. "There you go. That is now a fully functioning D.E.A. communication device."

"Thanks." I didn't pick it up. My gaze was on the .357 he had put back into his holster.

"Okay, Ms. Dai Break Jones, let's go over your dos and don'ts. Don't ever be without that phone. Do sell a lot of cocaine . . . and that's it for now."

"That's it?" I scooted my chair back from the table and picked up my phone.

"That's it. We will be in touch." Again he had that Thanksgiving Day smile on his face, and he gave me another wink.

I wasn't buying the smile or the wink.

"What happens if I get busted selling crack?" I was looking at my phone/slash snitch device when I asked the question.

"Don't worry. All of those issues are in our ball park. But do try your best not to commit any more noon day murders," Brent advised.

Still looking at my phone, I asked, "Don't I get to talk to a lawyer or something?"

"Why?" The sales clerk asked with attitude.

I put the phone back in my pocket and decided not to answer her 'why.'

"You are not under arrest or being detained. You don't need a lawyer. The less people that know about your situation the better. I don't think the people in your circle will understand you turning snitch. Do you?" She snapped her tool box shut. She looked up at me with German Shepherd eyes.

"Fuck you, a'ight? I ain't no damn snitch."

She raised her eyesbrows and opened her dog eyes wide and said, "Oh, but you are. You're either a snitch or a convict. And as a snitch, you need to get started selling crack."

I wanted to tell her about her butt ugly mama, and her piss po' ass daddy, but that wouldn't have been smart. These people was the Feds, and they had they attention on me and mine.

My 'Big Papa' ring tone went off, and her phone rang along with mine. She checked hers and said, "It's your daddy calling."

My phone was in my pocket, so I couldn't tell if it was my daddy or not, but her nasty tone caused me to give her the finger on the way out the door.

Outside, I checked my phone and it was my daddy. I answered it while walking through the parking lot, and immediately told him, "Daddy, my phone is bugged."

"Okay. By them local people or them people from Washington?"

"Them people from Washington. Just sat down with them and they told me about all thirty of them Cali birds."

"Did they now?"

"Yep, but they ain't hunting them birds, they trying to take these local people out to the reservation, using them Cali birds for bait."

"Really?"

"On everythang, Daddy."

"All right, dig this. Meet me and Duran tomorrow at three-fifteen in the afternoon. We coming in on American at Midway. We will talk more then, Midway not O'Hare."

"I got it, Daddy. See you then."

He didn't say a word about Duran's daddy, so I figured he was with the load. Those D.E.A. quacks must have been crazy if they thought I wasn't going to tell my daddy about the situation. Before I got into my truck I looked around to see what vehicles was around me. The fair headed boy said they had been following me for weeks. Nothing looked familiar.

Two things was on my mind: me on film committing murder, and my daddy getting home safe. I was happy he wasn't with the load, but it was him they mentioned in possession of the thirty kilos. Him, not Founder Aims.

"Damn! They got a pimp on tape."

I couldn't even start the truck for thinking about how fucked my situation was. There was no sense in saying what I shouldn't have done. It was done. Thugs was serving twenty years for murder, and those were cases put together by the Chicago P.D. My shit was through the D.E.A. I had never even thought about going to prison, or being a damn snitch.

I started the truck and drove off, because I saw the agents coming out of the Dunkin' Donuts. They were the last people in the damn city I wanted to talk to.

I was at the light on Thirty-fifth and King Drive when I heard, "Have a nice day, Dai Break Jones." It was Doodoo Brown's voice, and it came from my phone that was in my pocket. It didn't ring or click. His voice was just there. "Don't forget to pick your daddy up tomorrow from Midway, not O'Hare."

"I won't," I said, quietly.

"Good. Talk to you later."

I was in a trick bag for real, and a pimp needed to think. I drove back to the clubhouse to be around my clique.

*

At first, they didn't believe me. Then after they started believing, they got scared. Both of them started looking around for bugs and cameras in the clubhouse. When I told them about my phone, they stopped talking all together. Tray Six went outside to his white-on-white-in-white big-body Caddy, and brought back a spiral bound notebook and pens.

He handed us each a sheet of paper, and we started writing notes to each other. We agreed that all we could do was wait for Duran and Daddy to get back. They went back to playing the video game. I sat on the couch next to Benny Moon and pulled out my iPod. I scrolled to the first Nelly C.D. and clicked it on. Yeah, the situation hadn't changed, but I was with my people, and like my daddy says, 'Shared trouble, is trouble lessened.'

Chapter Eleven

Benny Moon woke me up by handing me an open box of shrimp fried rice with a pink plastic fork sticking out of it. The girls were up and sitting in the front room with us. The flat screen was on B.E.T., and Red Foxx was fussing at Lamont. The conversation between my girls, Benny Moon and Tray Six was about Aunt Ester.

They was arguing about whether she was really ugly or not. I said she wasn't ugly, because she reminded me of Tommy Locke's mother. No sooner than I had said it, I regretted opening my mouth because saying that put a damper on the whole mood. We all tried to talk around it, but my words took the happy mood.

"We all gonna miss him, ain't no sense in acting like we not." Benny Moon was on the end of the couch closest to the T.V. "We grew up with him. We all pissed in the same baby beds. He was our boy, one of five since birth . . . shit." He dropped heavily back against the couch, with his head on the wall. "Damn, shit, fuck it," he started crying and didn't try to hide the falling tears. My eyes went from him to the window. It was dark outside. I had slept for hours. I filled my mouth with the shrimp fried rice.

Pauline was next to me on the couch, and at my feet on the floor was Billie. They both got up and went into the front bedroom when Benny Moon started crying. Billie knew to leave when things got real with the clique.

"I-i-i-it just wasn't right. We could of h-h-h-helped him stop. We could have helped him!" Then he started crying and sniffing snot, and the next thing I knew I was dropping crocodile tears, too.

Benny Moon stood up and walked over to the flat screen and said,

"I went over to they house and saw that thugs had cleared the snow and started a little memorial with his picture and a couple of bottles. I added a bag of Harold's chicken and a fifth of Remy. It was a bunch of people adding stuff too, the front of they yard was getting filled up earlier."

Nobody said anything else.

A pimp stood up because I had enough on my brain. Tripping over crack smoking Tommy Locke was not on the agenda. It was too much going on in my life. I looked down at my big faced watch and saw it was after seven thirty. The plan was to go up to the Hyatt at four. Better late than never. Whatever deal the Chinese dude had with the limo driver, he was going to have with me.

I put on my red fox and walked to the front door. Over my shoulder I yelled, "Pauline, Billie, let's roll." To Tray Six and Benny Moon I said, "I'll see y'all before the airport. We all riding together, right?"

"Yep. Fo' sho," was the answer, but I don't know who gave it.

*

When we got to the Hyatt at McCormick Place I valet parked. Pulling up in the enclosed circle of the drive was too fly. It was snowing on the street behind us, but we got out of the truck in warmth, and on dry pavement. I told the knock-kneed attendant who was staring hard at my girls, "They working tonight, about to rent a suite. Stop on by when you get off."

He answered with, "You best talk to Jason soon as you get into your room. Extension 2228. Where Ty?"

I passed him a twenty with the keys and said, "He ain't coming tonight."

Stepping by me and climbing into my truck, he said, "Ya know we get a discount for looking out. Ask ya fat butt cutie didn't I steer them good business last night. Ty was supposed to look out tonight."

Sounded like he was asking for a free date. "I thought that was between y'all and Jason?"

"Nope. Not the side business that comes straight to the room; that's between us and Ty. And tonight I guess it will be between us and you."

Side business. That sounded good. "Ain't no problem, buddy. We gonna work it just fine."

I rented a two-bedroom suite with a wet bar. After seeing me talk so long with the parking attendant, the desk clerk gave me the nod, and I got the room for a hundred in her palm and two-eighty-five on the books. She registered me as Oliver Shortfellow, DD.S. It appeared the dentists' convention was booked to start that evening.

The suite was fly. There was a seating area with a couch, sleeper sofa, big chairs, and the bar in the middle. It had a desk with lap top and three flat screens. While the girls were walking around ohhing and ahhing, I dialed Jason's extension.

He answered with, "No Ty?"

"Nope he couldn't make it. Had to go out of town on an emergency."

"Did he explain the system?"

"Pretty much. You direct and I send."

"Yes, that's about it. I'm sending six girls over to you now. Things should be getting started in another hour. Are you working, too? You're a lesbian, right?"

He had obviously been told something about me either from the parking attendant or the desk clerk. "Only for a thousand or better." I purposely didn't answer the lesbian question.

"Men and women?"

"Only women."

"I got a man who likes Black women to stick rubber dicks up his butt. I can probably get him up to two grand, and your end will be fifteen hundred. Interested?"

Hearing him say that turned me on a little. The thought of fucking a man in his ass with a strap-on titillated me. I went as far as to picture the man. I saw Doodoo Brown, the D.E.A. agent, bent over a table in Dunkin' Donuts.

"Let me know. It might happen for fifteen-hundred."

"Oh, and I am sending up a limo driver's uniform for you. How you are dressed is inappropriate for the hotel. You are about a two extra large, right?"

"Right."

"Good. The girls are on they're way."

The six hens he sent brought the sizzle in with them. They came through the door dressed like downtown business women. But once the door closed, nothing but hooker came out they mouths. They talked about turning tricks from Beijing to Cairo, and they weren't bragging. It was all matter-of-fact.

It sounded like Jason was part of a larger network, controlled from Japan. He was Japanese, not Chinese, and there was a worker like him in every major city across the globe. In Vegas, the worker's name was Patrick; in Dallas, it was Jerome; in Montréal, it was Lawrence; in Paris, it was Daniel, and all the workers were Japanese.

From they buzzing conversation, I heard that each girl had started out in they home cities. Like my girls, they were working with a pimp, until they met the Japanese worker. Once the worker explained they operation, none of them hesitated in leaving they pimps. At that point in the conversation, each of the six sophisticated looking women turned to me in unison and laughed. They laughed at me.

Instantly, they well made up faces reminded me of being in the doughnut shop with the D.E.A. These stylish ho'es looked at me like I wasn't shit, just like the D.E.A. agents had done. None of them had pimps any longer, only travel agents. My girls tried to act like they weren't listening to the flashy talk, but they was. That was the shit that filled they heads the night before. What I should have done was left right then with my girls in tow, but the promise of big money held a pimp in place.

I was in the big bedroom of the suite changing into the driver's uniform, and my phone fell from my Coogi jeans pocket. That put the whole D.E.A. situation heavier on my mind. They had heard all my pimping business. I decided to leave the phone in the jeans because what was going on out there had nothing to do with selling crack. If they objected, I was sure they had a way to reach me.

Putting on the chauffer's uniform was kind of freaky, because it was just like the one Ty wore, with the little cap and everything. The phone rang inside my jeans.

It was my daddy's home number.

"Dai Break?"

"Hey, Cheryl."

"I just got a call from the hospital. Daisy is dead."

"What?"

"She's gone, Dai Break. She's gone."

111

"Gone where? What are you talking about?"

"She is dead. She died in the hospital."

"How?"

"She's gone. Something about fluid in her lungs. You got to send somebody for the body."

"Huh?"

"Her body has to be picked up by a funeral parlor."

"What?"

"Never mind. I'll handle it when your daddy gets home. Goodbye."

After she hung up, a pimp thought I heard her wrong. I tried to call her back, but my fingers wouldn't move. They wouldn't push the buttons, nor would they hold the phone. The phone fell to the floor, but I couldn't bend down for it.

My body was stuck. I was unable to move. When I leaned forward, a pimp fell to the bed on top my clothes.

Something was wrong with my stomach. It was tightening up and making breathing hard. A smoke detector went off, too. But when I covered my ears, I realized the sound was inside my head. A pimp tried to stand, but I couldn't push myself up from the bed. Couldn't even roll over. I tried to yell for my girls, but nothing came out my mouth. I couldn't turn my head or take my hands from my ears.

When Pauline came into the room, I saw her screaming, but a pimp couldn't hear a sound because the smoke detector was still going off in my head. After her, other people came into the room, but all I could do was look at them.

I saw the ambulance people come in and put me on a stretcher. When they rolled me past the dresser mirror, I saw that I hadn't put the uniform pants on. I was in my boxer briefs and they didn't cover me up. They rolled me out just like I was, knees up, in my drawers, with my hands stuck on my ears.

In the ambulance, the female attendant covered me up and tried to talk to me, but I couldn't hear shit, just the alarm in my head. I tried to close my eyes, but couldn't. I saw her give me a shot, but didn't feel the prick. I felt my hands drop from my ears. The ringing stopped and my eyes closed.

*

Part of my mind knew I was sleeping and didn't want to wake up. The other part wanted to wake up just to see what happened. I remember thinking that if I stayed asleep the cozy feeling would stay. Something bad was waiting for me if I woke up, something that would hurt my daddy, something that would make me leave home; so I tried not to wake up. Floating in sleep land was better than . . . being in Dunkin' Donuts with the D.E.A. It was better than something else, too, but that wouldn't come to my mind. The cozy feeling was interrupted by somebody screaming for they uniform.

The place that formed around me was the block where I had shot the limo driver. The voice I heard was his. He was running down the sunny block, past the parked cars and gray stone homes, towards me. He was in my boxer briefs, screaming for his uniform. When I looked down at myself, I had on the chauffer's outfit with the little cap in hand.

The closer he got, the clearer I saw him. His forehead was cracked open, and bits of it were falling to the snow-covered sidewalk. I stood stuck, unable to move out of his path. He ran up on me, but when he got to me, he wasn't the limo driver. He was Tommy Locke, and he

113

said, "One to the head because you already dead." Then he put a gun to my head.

At that point, I forced my eyes open.

I looked around and saw the hospital room. Then the other thing that made sleep land better than reality came to my mind. Daisy was dead. My bottom bitch was dead. The thought took my breath away.

My pretty, too fine to be a ho'e, sweet girl was dead. I thought about the first night I saw her at my birthday party, even then I thought she was star . . . and she was. That ho'e made my money. Damn, a pimp is gonna miss her.

I tried to sit up, because if I laid still, the tears would come. I had felt them welling in my eyes. It wasn't time to cry. It was time to find out how she died. It was time to find out what went wrong with her treatment. It was time to find out who killed her.

First, I tried to move my right arm and couldn't. My left arm wouldn't budge either. It was the same with my legs. I couldn't twist or turn. There were no straps holding me, but I couldn't move. I cleared my throat and called, "Nurse." At least I could talk and hear.

When the little old white lady nurse came in, she must have saw the panic in my eyes, because she immediately told me, "It's only temporary, dear. The doctor said something has over-loaded your central nervous system. The more you sleep, the better."

She came over to me and fluffed my pillow and gave me a shot. I didn't feel the needle, but a pimp felt the effects of the drug. I returned to sleep land.

I was a kid, maybe about five years old, and I had pissed in the bed. Too afraid to call for my daddy, I stood in the room crying, because I didn't know what to do. Laying in the wet bed was not an option, and if I turned on the light and went to the bathroom, my daddy would wake up. So I stood in the dark crying.

Then I heard my daddy. He was standing in the dark doorway. "Gangsters don't cry about things. They fix them. Go wash up, then come back and take those pissy sheets off your bed and put some clean ones on it. And tomorrow night, don't drink a whole can of pop before you go to bed. You pissed the bed because you drank too much before you went to sleep. Fix your problems, Dai Break, don't cry about them."

When I woke up, a pimp realized I couldn't fix Daisy being dead, so I cried.

Chapter Twelve

The old white lady nurse must have told them I was awake, because at the foot of my bed is Doodoo Brown and Brent. Surprisingly, I am able to raise my arm and cover my eyes due to one of them switching on the ceiling lights.

Doodoo Brown says, "Sorry about Daisy. We know she was important to you."

I don't answer. I try to move my other arm and it responds, too. And so do my legs, feet and toes. A pimp is back in action. I sit up with ease.

"How did she die, do you know?" I ask.

"Pneumonia is what we were told"

"Where am I, what hospital is this?"

"You are on the Southside, close to your daddy. We let the hospital staff notify him today. He's on his way up here with some of the other members of the E.O.G. Oh, and to update you further, your other two ump, ump . . . working girls, shall we say? Well, they left town this morning with a group of high class hookers, and I must say, they seemed to fit right in. Here, I got a shot of them boarding the plane."

He comes up to me and again he flips open the phone, and on the screen, I see Billie and Pauline handing the airline attendant boarding passes. Billie is smiling, and pulling a little suit case on wheels behind her. The ho'e has my red fox jacket draped over her shoulders. When Pauline passes the podium, she looks back over her shoulder, like she's expecting somebody to call her back, but she steps through the door behind Billie. Two of the hens from the hotel follow her. My hos are jumping ship, but they did look damn good in those business suits.

Daisy would have looked good in one too.

"Now . . . no more distractions, Dai Break Jones. It's time to get started selling cocaine. Don't forget."

He replays the loop of me shooting the limo driver.

"You're with us now. Oh, and we brought your clothes and phone from the hotel. I wouldn't want you to forget your life line." He holds up a gym bag with my stuff in it. "Your buddy, Duran, hasn't been wasting any time. Looks like your father has left the distribution to him and your clique. That's good for you." He sighs and stretches. "You will be released tomorrow morning. Talk to you soon." He pats me on the thigh, winks and leaves.

Black bastard. I hope he chokes to death on rat shit. I swing my legs to the side of the bed and slide my feet down to the floor. A pimp stands with no problem. On the toilet, I piss hard, like a race horse, causing the cool bowl of water to splash the back of my thighs. I can't remember the last time I made water.

Looks like the pimp game is over, at least for now. In the shower my mind goes to my daddy. He will know what my next move should be. Him and Duran probably already got this whole situation figured out.

I walk out of the bathroom to find the agent with the German Shepherd eyes sitting in the chair under the television. She's got on skin tight pink short shorts, a white sports bra, and white four inch spike heels. In her lap is a white rabbit jacket. Her blond hair has been slicked down, and her dog eyes were lined with black eye shadow and pencil. She looks like a real ho'e.

I don't have to ask. It is obvious. I must have caused doubt because they put her ass on me.

117

"So, you turning tricks?" I say, walking past her to the bed.

"In your fuckin' dreams. I'm here to oversee and expedite this operation. Your little breakdown has people concerned."

I stop with my back to her.

"Oh, so you the overseer? What does that make me?"

I tuck in the sheet and thin blanket at the bottom of the bed.

"That makes you the snitch."

I stop tucking the covers and spread my gown open, showing the bitch my ashy ass. I fart loud and long.

"Snitch that, bitch."

A thug climbs back into the bed, and under the thin blanket and sheet.

Jumping out of the chair, she screams, "You uncouth barbarian. How could you? Oh, my God, it stinks!" Her pretty rabbit jacket falls to floor.

She and the fart give me a much needed laugh. One that wets my eyes and causes me to fart some more. I cut loose so many that Shepherd Eyes breaks out the door.

When she comes back into the small room, she's armed with a plastic bottle of baby powder, and is puffing out powdery clouds in my direction. I could fart more, but the ones I dropped still have the room ripe, and a thug don't want to be embarrassed when my daddy and them get up here.

Standing at the foot of the wobbly bed with a hand over her nose, Shepherd Eyes squeaks out, "You and I are joined at the hip from now until this operation is over. We don't separate unless it's a must-do occurrence, and such situations should not be generated by you. Understand? We are joined at the hip!"

She is trying to stare me down to make a point.

I start to tell her to get the fuck out, but she can't. Shepherd Eyes has to do as she's told, too, just like me. This situation ain't giving her a choice, either.

"My daddy ain't gonna talk in front of you."

She picks her jacket up from the floor, "In cases like that the phone will do with me in the next room."

I remind myself that D.E.A. wants the crooked dope selling cop; not me or my daddy. Her goal is to get to Forrest, and my goal is to make that happen.

"So, after y'all get this Forrest guy, what happens with me?"

She sits back under the T.V.

"Don't know. That is out of my pay grade."

"So you like a soldier, huh? Not really a shot-caller?"

"That is correct. I make no decisions."

"Just a grunt, and you supposed to be undercover as my new ho'e, huh? I hope you know the clique members are going to want some of that white pussy."

I say 'pussy' real nasty stretching the 'u,' and then I hump my hips a couple of times, and send her a wink of my own.

"They like white girls. You ever been with a big Black man? I'm talking about a packing brother. You know thugs got big ones. Can you handle a big Black man? You look kind of narrow in the hips. Dressing the part, and living the part is two different things. It's easy to look like a ho'e, but can you *be* a ho'e?"

The tips of her ears are turning red and her nostrils are flaring.

"I'm not undercover as a prostitute. You will introduce me as your new lover, one you can't stand to be away from."

119

"Oh, yeah, my lover. Then I'ma want some of that white pussy."

I ain't smiling when I say it. Put a serious mack tone in my words to try and rattle her.

"Look, understand this, snitch. We are not playing games here. If I feel threatened at anytime, I will act as a trained D.E.A. agent and address the threat."

"Oh, so you like girly girls, huh?"

"That is not a point of concern for you, snitch."

"I now already told my daddy about y'all. He's going to know you a Fed."

"So, all the easier. As long as Lieutenant Forrest isn't aware, you won't have a problem."

"You can't just all of a sudden be part of my everyday life."

"Oh, but I am. Get used to it."

As she says that, my daddy, Duran and Benny Moon walk in. And they bring the cold weather in with them. I feel the chill of the air surrounding them.

They are dressed in black overcoats, suits and hats. They are all smiling until they see dog eyes.

"Hi," she says, sounding like a little girl, "I'm Vicki."

She gets no reply, and the smiles leave all they faces.

My daddy has on his black beaver hat, which he seldom wears. Benny Moon has a suit bag over his shoulder, and Duran has a shoe box in his hands. My Daddy has my black mink in his arms. Duran opens the shoe box, and I see a new pair of black 'gators, size eight, my size.

"We have funerals to attend," my daddy says. "Get dressed. You out of here. We will meet you out in the hall." They drop the coat, shoes, and suit bag on my bed and leave.

I turn my head to Vicki and say, "You can't go to a Black people's funeral dressed like that."

"I have other clothes." She goes to the closet and wrestles out a suit case, "At the hip, Dai Break Jones.. We are joined at the hip."

*

None of them seem surprised that Vicky gets in the stretch-limo with me. I sit between daddy and Duran, on the back seat. She takes a seat on the side bench to daddy's left, between Benny Moon and his brother, Heart.

To Heart, I say, "So, you one of this five?"

"Yep," he answers grinning from ear to ear. The boy been hoping to be one of us since he was a little kid. "Welcome, did you get the blessing I left you?"

"Yep. Benny gave it to me two days ago. Love that Dai Break."

"I figured you would. It's good to have you part of us."

We all throw up a E in his direction and say, "Blessed!"

Well, everyone but Vicky, who flinched with the greeting.

My daddy reached inside his coat pocket and pulls out a ball of tissue paper and hands it to Heart.

Heart unwraps a half-carat stud earring.

Benny Moon takes the gold Rolex foo his wrist and gives it to his brother. Duran passes him a dollar sign money clip, tight with hundreds.

Tray Six passes him a chrome plated .9 mm with a white pearl handle. They waited till I got out to bless him.

My Daddy tells the driver to pull over and to get out. My daddy

121

gets out, too, and calls Vicky with him. She looks confused, but gets out.

We five are alone in the back of the stretch. Duran holds up the thumb. I hold up the first finger, Benny Moon the second, Tray Six the third, and Heart the fourth.

"We are five before man and the hand of the Creator. Blessed," We all say. Then we all lower our heads in prayer.

I haven't prayed in years, because I am not sure who the prayers go to or that it does any good. I don't pray because I make goals. I get things done in my life.

Instead of closing my eyes in prayer, I look at my clique. I think about Daisy being dead. I remember the loop of my ho'es getting on the plane, and then I look down at my new alligator shoes. The people in this limo are my life, and I will live it until I die.

"We are one," Duran says. We all clap and nod toward Heart.

Duran pulls a chrome .45 from his black trench coat and hands it to me. "Figured you was naked getting out of the hospital and all."

"Love that about you, my brother." I place the pistol in the small of my back.

"So, she the Feds your daddy told us about?" Duran asked.

"D.E.A."

"And they after this cop, but they got you on tape doing a fool?"

"Yep."

"You know your daddy got you on this?"

"I hope so, 'cause I ain't got me."

Tray Six opens the Limo door calling my daddy, the driver, and Vicki back in.

*

122

Both services are being held at Gatlin's, on Halsted. Tommy Locke is in temple one, and my daddy scheduled Daisy's service to start directly after his, in temple two. When we walk into temple one, it is packed to the walls with E.O.G. members, and they are all dressed in black.

We wear black to funerals and white to weddings. We have filled this space. Thugs are pressed against the back and side walls. When my daddy walks in, everybody that's sitting, stands. I follow him to the front where seats have been held for him and me. The other founders are with they wives. It's always me and my daddy, regardless of who his live-in girlfriend is.

The preacher is the blind Reverend Jules. He does most of the E.O.G. funerals. Daddy says he was one of the most cold hearted gangsters in the city, until the police shot and killed his twelve year old son. He told daddy that Jesus came to him the same time his son was being gunned down, and called him to be a preacher, while he was driving to buy a new Cadillac. He accepted Christ right then. Ten minutes later, he got word about his son. He reached for his pistol and the Lord took his sight. He has been blind and a man of God every since. And he is the only preacher my daddy trusts.

Founder Locke is sitting on the corner of the first row of seats with Tommy Locke's mother on his side. I wonder if she knows he killed they son for E.O.G. law. It's a question I will never ask anyone.

The preacher's sermon is about Abraham. That is one of the few bible stories I know. Benny Moon's mama read it to us when we were kids. She said Abraham's story was important since Jews, Christians and Muslims called him father.

The preacher is talking about Abraham's love for his son, and how his love for God was greater. Abraham was going to kill his son for God, but God stopped him. My daddy wouldn't kill me for the love of God, or the love of E.O.G. That I know, but Founder Locke did kill his son for E.O.G. law. God took the preacher's sight for getting ready to kill for his son. God told Abraham not to kill his son, but Reverend Jules' son did die, and Founder Locke killed his son. None of it makes sense.

Tommy Locke is in that closed black casket in front of us, and his mama is sitting next to the man who put him in the casket.

None of it makes sense.

My daddy wouldn't kill me. I wouldn't kill him, and Tommy Locke's daddy shouldn't have killed him, either. I look at his mother and start crying. Somebody should tell her that her son's daddy killed him. Somebody should tell that E.O.G. didn't stop him like God did Abraham. Somebody should tell her that he was a crack-head, and got two to the head because he was already dead.

I should tell her something.

But I don't. The choir starts to sing and I can't stop crying.

My daddy puts his arm around me and says, "Easy, Dai Break. Take a breath, baby."

Something is going on with me. I don't cry like this. I ain't soft like this. Something is wrong, because a thug like me don't cry. It must be the drugs from the hospital. They must still be in my system, messing with my thoughts and my feelings.

The truth is Tommie knew the law; so much so that he tried to hide his crack smoking. He got caught, and that's why he is dead. His daddy had to kill him. It's E.O.G. law and I know it, but for some reason part of me still wants to cry out that his death was wrong, and tell his

124

mother the sin of his father.

I want to tell the preacher that Founder Locke is not like Abraham, and that he had no love for his son, only love for E.O.G. I want to scream in the mother's face that the father killed they son. I want to tell everybody that Tommy Locke was murdered by his daddy.

I immediately stand to leave, because I am not right in my thoughts. It is more than me inside my head. Going up the left aisle, I see the surprised look on soldiers' faces; none of them have ever seen a tear in my eye. I push my way out, and into the large lobby area. I spot the ladies room and head straight for it. I go into a stall and begin wailing. This ain't me, but I can't stop it. I feel so sad for Tommy and his mama. The moans and groans are foreign to my ears, but the need for them is all up in my heart. I collapse to the floor with my back against the toilet and sob.

"So, you crying for her now. I knew it was going to happen. No woman with a heart can take such a loss. That girl loved you, she loved you hard. And you killed her. You killed her, Dai Break Jones. Daisy's blood is on your hands. Your daddy, or no other soul, can carry that for you. Pray while you down there, girl. Pray that the Lord will forgive you for murdering one of his.

"That child had a good heart, Dai Break, and breaking it wasn't enough for you. You had to kill her. Well, you better pray that Jesus finds you a way to the Lord's forgiveness."

It is Cheryl standing above me.

"The doctors killed her, not me. They let her out of the hospital too soon. It was the doctors."

"Lord, help this child," she says standing over me, shaking her head and dropping tears.

125

"It wasn't me!" I stand up from the toilet and grab her by her mink collar, "You crazy if you think it was me." I push her across the bathroom and pin her head against the mirror, "I ain't killed nobody!" I pull the .45 from the small of my back and put it to her head.

"You killed Daisy, and shooting me ain't going to change that. You did a murder. You killed somebody that loved you!"

I jack the .45 and put one in the chamber. I scream at her, "No, not me. It's founder Locke, not me. I ain't a murderer. He is. I didn't kill nobody. He killed Tommie Locke! The doctors killed Daisy! I ain't kill nobody!"

I start banging Cheryl's head against the mirror when someone pulls me away from her and slings me to the floor. I hit the floor with a bang, a loud blast that rings in my ears. A thug looks up from the floor to see Vicki's dog eyes and her pistol in my face.

"Calm the fuck down," she seems to be yelling, but I can barely hear her and she is saying more stuff, but now I really don't hear her. Cheryl is standing next to her, and her face looks like she's screaming and pointing her finger at me. Something warm is on my stomach. I put my hand on it and feel the wetness. Bringing my hand up, I see it's covered in blood.

"Daddy. Get my daddy."

I want to say something more, but my mouth is filling with blood. I try to spit it out, but I can't catch a good breath.

I see my daddy pushing his way to me. He is down on his knees next to me. He pulls me up into his arms and holds me tight. Not since I was a little girl has he held me so. I love my daddy, and my daddy loves me. If I could, I would stay with him always, but I know I can't. A light is behind his head, a damn bright light.

In the corner above the light, it looks like I see Tommie Locke, and Daisy. He's waving at me to follow. She's only smiling. I am not trying to catch my breath anymore. I exhale.

*

I inhale and exhale and inhale. My mouth is blood free. When my eyes open, Benny Moon's mother is in my face. Her eyes are deep in mine. Her thumbs are pressed against my forehead. Her words are gibberish, and the look on her face is feverish. I am strapped down to a gurney in the back of an ambulance. There are no attendants, just Benny Moon's mama and my daddy.

"Quiet, child, don't talk, only breath. Sleep, baby. Sleep now."

*

I wake up to my daddy's voice, "If she dies, everybody in here dies. I swear to God." It's not Benny Moon's mother I see, but Dr. Silverman. It is cold in the room.

*

There is a tube up my nose. Bandages are wrapped around the middle of my body and an I.V. is in my arm. My daddy and Benny Moon's mama are in chairs asleep. This ain't a hospital room.

*

"She will be on dialysis for the rest of her life. It's a miracle that she is alive, Mr. Jones. A miracle I had very little to do with. She was pronounced dead at the scene. D.O.A. for here. There should be no problem with the death certificate. And the body for cremation was picked by the funeral home you sent."

"How much did you say?"

"We agreed on two hundred thousand, Mr. Jones."

"Duran, pay the man."

127

I hear, but I can't open my eyes to see.

*

It was the morgue. They kept me in the morgue for three days. That's where the doctor kept me hid after I arrived. The world thinks I'm dead, the D.E.A. included. I was cremated yesterday, and Duran told me the D.E.A. and Chicago P.D. tried to stop the service, but they got there five minutes too late.

Duran said I was dead, but Benny Moon's mama brought me back. He said he saw my guts on the bathroom floor. He said the .45 blew a hole in my stomach big enough to pass a volley ball through. Judging by my bandages, I believe him.

Dr. Silverman and my daddy zipped me up in the body bag that I am in now. The only way they could get me out of the hospital unnoticed, was in a hearse. So I am in a body bag, on a gurney, being rolled out to a hearse at three o'clock in the morning.

*

On the little airplane, it's the pilot, me and Duran. I am laying on a cot on the floor of the plane, and Duran is sitting next to me on a pillow. There are seats, but I still can't sit up.

"My mama said you are going to like it there."

"I doubt that. What kind of life will I have in Columbia?"

Riding on this little plane is as bumpy as riding the city bus. If I wasn't strapped down to this cot, and it secured to the floor, I would have rolled away awhile ago. Duran is holding onto floor straps, too.

"It's a big city, Dai Break, not a village. It's not that different from Chicago."

"I don't speak Spanish."

My stomach, or what's left of it, hurts bad. I haven't seen what is under the bandages. My daddy said doctors will be waiting for me when we land, and I will be going back to a hospital.

"You will learn like I did. When you hear it every day it sinks in. Besides, you won't be there forever, and it's better than prison."

I can barely see his face in the dim light of the plane. He sounds tired and worried, but he's trying to cheer me up. Better than prison, life on dialysis, and probably a piss and shit bag for the rest of my life; better than prison?

"You are alive, Dai Break, and you need to be grateful for that." He talks like he's reading my mind.

"How long are you going to be over here with me?"

"Not long. Just until my mother and Cheryl come over. They are going to set up your house, and find you a good nurse. I got work to do here. We got the load in without a hitch, despite the D.E.A. If you wouldn't have warned us, things could have been real fucked up. Everybody says that. You did good."

My daddy begged me to let Cheryl fly with me tonight, but I refused. He said she's blaming herself for the gun going off, and it's tearing her up. I think she's sweating for her life, and faking concern for me. But I don't want her with me, because what she said in the bathroom was the truth. I did kill Daisy, but shit . . . that was the game we played. I can only feel so sad about it.

"You got them pain pills?"

Duran pulls a little bottle from his jeans pocket and puts two pills into my palm. He caps the pill bottle and uncaps his water bottle and helps me down the medicine.

I am not going to trip over Daisy. I lost my home, my life, and my health. My daddy said no more than eight years in Columbia, but when

129

I come back, I won't be able to come back to Chicago. I'll have to come back as a Columbian immigrant with a new identify. He said we will probably live in Atlanta. In the meantime, I am to assist E.O.G. from Columbia, as low key as possible. No one knows what I will do, but like Duran said, it's better than prison. And at least I am alive.

AUG 1 - 2016

CPSIA information can be obtained at www.ICGtesting.com
Printed in the USA
LVOW08s1516230616

493837LV00002B/225/P